A Family for Andi
Eileen Berger

Love Inspired®

Published by Steeple Hill Books

STEEPLE HILL BOOKS

Steeple
Hill™

ISBN 0-373-87057-4

A FAMILY FOR ANDI

Copyright © 1999 by Eileen M. Berger

Printed in U.S.A.

She raised her hand to ring the bell, but the door opened and he was there....

Andi walked inside—and into his arms. No words were spoken, none needed. Her face was buried against his shoulder and neck, his cheek against her hair.

So this is what it's like to come home to Keith.

She had no idea how long they remained like that. It was she who finally forced herself to draw away as his hands moved slowly down her arms, taking her hands in his.

How could I have let this happen? What have I done?

"I'm sorry...." She didn't want to look into his beautiful brown eyes, which could show such tenderness.

He lifted her chin with one finger. "Look at me, sweetheart. Please... It's all right. Don't be afraid."

It's not you I don't trust. I had no idea that in one short week I could fall in love! With a man whom there's no chance of my marrying!

And I've been so completely dishonest with you!

EILEEN BERGER

has been writing for many years, mostly children's stories and poetry when her daughter and two sons were small, before having hundreds of other manuscripts published. She had been happy growing up on a farm, then living for a time in two major American cities, but feels blessed to continue living in the same north-central Pennsylvania town, Hughesville, where she and her husband, Bob, raised their now-grown children.

She is active in writing circles as speaker, teacher, board member, panelist, conference director and contest coordinator, but is especially grateful for the West Branch Christian Writers, the wonderful critique/support group without which she says she might never have got even the first of her six novels published.

Ask and it will be given you;
seek and you will find;
knock and the door will be
opened to you.

For everyone who asks receives;
he who seeks finds;
and to him who knocks
the door will be opened.

—*Matthew* 7:7-8

To Bob,
the man I love more than life itself.
No *wonder* I like writing romances!

Chapter One

Andrea Barker lowered the hood of her secondhand car, hoping she'd followed the mechanic's instructions correctly. She knew little about motors, and her intention was not to fix this one but to make it break down.

She was limping more than usual, but should have expected that; she'd not tried driving long distances since the accident.

The trip from Chicago had been taxing, even though she stayed overnight in Ohio and stopped every few hours to walk a while. Now, getting back in the car, she massaged her right knee and leg before pulling the door shut, fastening the seat belt, and turning the ignition key.

The engine started, and Andi smiled. She was here in Pennsylvania. She took a moment to check her appearance in the rearview mirror before pulling out onto the highway—and resisted the urge to run a comb through her below-shoulder-length auburn hair or to apply color to her fairly full lips. The blue eyes looking back at her sparkled with anticipation.

There *was* a strange grinding sound, but the car handled fine, as the man who cared for their vehicles had promised.

Hurdle number one taken care of!

If only the rest would go this smoothly! Dad, though apparently understanding her concerns, had argued against her "harebrained scheme," but she'd been adamant. "I really want to meet my cousins—get to know them. I realize there's been an estrangement ever since your mother left when still in her teens, but..."

"They treated her very badly, Andi."

"But that was a previous generation. Hopefully this one's better."

"I don't want you hurt like your grandmother was."

"Well, someone's got to find out about them—at least how they handle what money they have now and what they'd likely do with a windfall, that sort of thing."

"You think they won't be on their best behavior with you there?" His heavy brows came almost together in that way that used to make her fidget before she learned to recognize the difference between frowns of concentration and those of disapproval.

"They'll have no reason to be suspicious."

He sat there shaking his head. "You've always liked fantasies, romances, and other not-for-real stuff. I'm afraid, my dear, that what you're proposing falls into one of those categories. You expect to invade the town of Sylvan Falls, observe our relatives, win their confidence, and determine within a few days if giving them a large sum of money is a sound idea?''

When put like that, it did sound like an ambitious undertaking. ''I don't expect to accomplish it in a couple of days.'' That had been months after the death of Jon—Jonathan William Bascomb III—and she was still on crutches, emotionally as well as physically. They'd grown up together and had been in the same grade from preschool through ninth—until his grandparents had enrolled him at Madison Academy to prepare for an Ivy League education.

Andi stayed in public schools, but they remained good friends. Even while he was at Yale and she at Michigan State, they had long conversations on the phone and were often together during holiday and summer breaks.

But then, on his twenty-first birthday, he came into that inheritance from his paternal grandmother—and things were never the same. ''Jon would be alive today if it weren't for all that money!'' Andi had cried out as she sat with Dad in his den. ''He had no conception of what to do with it—what he *should* do with it.''

''You must admit that most of his folks' decisions have been good ones, Andi. The academy. Yale...''

''But he'd never handled money—*much* money. Whatever he wanted, he bought—the sailboat, the sports car, *every*thing. And he was so generous and loving, always doing for others...''

Tears filled her eyes, remembering the plane he'd chartered to take twenty-seven friends to Paris last fall, to help celebrate his twenty-seventh birthday. And the diamond necklace he had insisted that she accept last Christmas. "And that led to disaster when his new 'friends' proved only too eager to help spend his wealth."

Her father leaned back, raising the footrest of his cordovan leather recliner. His glance circled the big room, with its thousands of books, and all those snapshots of Andi, showing her eyes, fair coloring and regular features to be much like his own, though more feminine. "You're convinced twenty-one's too young for that much responsibility?"

"If a person hasn't had experience with money, *any* age may be 'too young.' I appreciate your insisting that I learn about finance and investing—but Jon's inability to handle it makes me concerned about our Pennsylvania cousins. I don't want others destroyed by receiving large amounts."

She leaned forward to look into his clear dark blue eyes. "I know we've discussed giving a sizable amount up front, with the rest in trust funds, but if they should be mean-spirited people whose love of money hurts them or others, even *that's* no favor."

She knew her father was a soft touch, and some found it easy to take advantage of his generosity. She almost reminded him about Mother's only cousin, Lynne. They'd helped her out of two major jams—if they hadn't, she'd have been in jail for years. But they made it clear that second time that there'd be no more money from them, *ever*.

Jon's being killed was almost too painful to think about. Andi had known the inevitability of Mother's death from cancer while she was a junior in college—but not Jon!

Dad had not been thrilled at the possibility of hav-

ing Jon as a son-in-law, but he grieved with—or for—
her. She noticed he'd made changes in his own life
since then—losing that extra twenty pounds, cutting
out smoking, watching what he ate, and exercising
regularly.

She understood his urgency when speaking of up-
dating his will, of making all those changes. "I'm
glad you're setting up the Barker Foundation, Dad,"
she assured him, "and I'm all for the endowments to
our alma maters and gifts to other schools and charities. But I'm concerned about your leaving so much
to The Cousins." She'd never thought of them as individuals, with personalities. "What effect might sudden wealth have on them?"

He pursed his lips. "Would you feel better if I
hired a private detective? There's a good one I've
used."

"I hope you didn't have him checking on my
friends." It was a statement, not a question, and he
neither denied nor confirmed it. Actually, she'd prefer
not knowing if he'd investigated Jon. Or others. "Perhaps he *could* get basic information, since all we
know is names."

"I do know more than that, though nothing about
what makes them tick, or how they handle finances."
He rubbed his square jaw with his palm. "We don't
have many to check, since my family wasn't very
prolific. Including us."

She reached from her high-backed chair to place a
hand on his forearm. "At least you had me."

"Impossible to forget we were blessed with the
best." Smiling, he covered her hand with his. "As
you know, I'm Katherine's only child, and MaryJean

is the only cousin in my generation—though she's about fifteen years older.

"Her father, Michael, and my mother were brother and sister, but had no real relationship—not even letters back and forth, or phone calls. I never met him nor his daughter, but did learn that MaryJean's husband, Philip McHenry, died some years ago, leaving his wife and three grown children, who'd be your second cousins.

"They all live in or near Sylvan Falls..."

As they were finishing dinner a week later, Dad handed her a thick folder. Pushing aside her half-eaten strawberry sherbet, she riffled through the annotated sheets containing information on the McHenrys. "You've *read* all this?"

"Just skimmed. It arrived just before this morning's staff meeting, and I had appointments all day."

Until recently she'd been unaware of how demanding his schedule was, and how thoroughly he knew the workings of each department in the electronics company he'd founded. Now that she was here, learning the business, she had a new appreciation of both his leadership ability and acumen.

She'd agreed that she must become familiar with the work and staff of each section, but the experience was challenging. As "the boss's kid," she'd found herself pampered, ignored or fawned over—all of which she detested.

"Dad, I want to leave for a while...."

"That's not a good idea, Andi. Neither for the department's sake nor for yours."

"I'll be back soon."

The right corner of his mouth quirked upward. "You *could* find you enjoy freedom more than on-the-job training."

"I do enjoy what I'm doing, and know how necessary it is if I'm to become your assistant." And I think you're at least partly teasing, she thought. "You certainly guessed this wouldn't satisfy my curiosity. Actually, it whets my desire for personal contact." She tapped one sheet with a forefinger. "It says here that MaryJean runs a bed-and-breakfast. If I'm lucky, perhaps I can stay there."

"Nobody there probably knows I exist," she said after they'd discussed a number of things that would have to be arranged, "but, just in case, I'll need an assumed name, address and other identification."

He looked at her over his glasses. "You've given this appreciable thought."

"Yes. I have." There must be no slipups, nothing carelessly left undone. "By the time I finish my time in Accounts Receivable, I hope to come up with a good reason for being there—and a way to stretch my time till I get all the information I want."

So here she was, on a beautiful, hot Saturday, the tenth of June, driving around a curve, looking down on the Norman Rockwell-like town of Sylvan Falls. Since there was little traffic, Andi proceeded slowly enough to take in the regular grid of tree-lined streets.

Turning right onto Main Street, she glanced at the dashboard clock—5:23. All *right*. The garage was supposed to be here on North Main, and they'd probably not check her car till Monday.

Uneven numbers on the left side…500 block, 400s. Ah, *there* it was: McHenry Auto!

She paused for two northbound vehicles before crossing over into the lot where row after row of new and used cars, vans and trucks stood parked to her right. With little space for parking, she stopped beside a sporty, brightly polished new red pickup, satisfied that no one could mistake her dusty, purchased-for-this-trip, six-year-old vehicle as being offered for sale.

One of the three huge rolling doors along the side of the building was open and clearly marked, but she decided to enter through the glassed-in showroom facing the street. A bell jangled as she opened the door, and a loud buzzer sounded beyond the rear wall. She glanced around, smiling, already conscious of differences between Chicago and this small town.

A sparkling luxury sedan, a minivan, and two compact models were displayed in the spotless room. Good setup, she decided, walking between two of them. The rear door on the left swung open and a tall, brown-eyed man in tan, grease-smeared coveralls came toward her, wiping his hands with a towel. "I'm Keith. How can I help you?"

This couldn't be her cousin, could it? *That* Keith was supposed to be an engineer. "My car, that blue hatchback out there—" pointing "—has been making a strange noise, and I thought…" Her voice trailed off.

"How long has it been doing that?"

"Not very long. And I realize it's late."

He nodded. "Especially for a Saturday."

She tried to sound concerned; he must not suspect

this to be what she wanted to hear. "I hesitated to drive much farther, the way it sounds."

He listened with a thoughtful expression. An attractive thoughtful expression, Andi decided. "You're right, but there's no way it can be looked at today. There's only one mechanic here this late, and he's finishing up an emergency job. I know he's got to get home."

"What about you?" Why did I ask that? she wondered. I don't want anyone doing it today!

"Sorry. I have a date in Dalton for—" a quick glance at the wall clock "—an hour from now. I can't be late."

"Oh." He didn't look apologetic, and she told herself that her momentary feeling of being a little sorry that he had a date was sheer foolishness. But he *was* incredibly handsome and had such a warm, friendly smile. "Well, is there anywhere nearby where I might stay till it's taken care of?"

"That I can help with." His warm hand under her bare elbow steered her toward the window. "See that big white house across the street, three doors down, with the big front porch? That's my grandmother's, and she rents rooms—though her sign's too small to read from here, isn't it?"

So Keith is my cousin, she thought. "It looks nice." 'Nice' was such a weak word, but she couldn't let him know how much more this was than she'd feared.

"If you'd like, I can walk over with you."

"I'd appreciate that."

After stepping back into the garage to explain about the car parked in the lot, Keith walked Andi to her car, where they collected the worn suitcase and garment bag she'd brought. "And you want your laptop, don't you?" he asked, lifting the leather case.

"Yes, please." She handed him the keys for the car before locking the doors. "I'd better introduce myself, since you're taking me to meet your grandmother. I'm Anne Marker—and generally answer to 'Annie.'" That's close enough to 'Andi Barker' that I should respond when spoken to, she told herself.

"Pleased to meet you, Annie Marker. I'm Keith McHenry, son of the founder and owner of McHenry Auto."

"Hello." Their shared smiles made up for the lack of a handshake. "You work here with your father?"

"I used to, some, while going to school—but now it's just to bring in my own vehicles and service them. Actually, I'm an engineer with a design group in Dalton."

She stopped on the sidewalk, and he turned to look at her. "Were you finished? I shouldn't take you away if you have to go somewhere."

"You worry too much, Annie," he said lightly. "You came at the right time. I'm about to go home and clean up."

Better timing than you can imagine! she thought. As they crossed the street, several people in cars tooted or waved. "You're a popular guy, Keith. You seem to know everyone in town," Andi remarked.

His chuckle was deep-throated. "I do. But I think they're all making such a racket because they're not accustomed to seeing me with such a gorgeous woman."

He probably thought she was flirting, she realized.

She concentrated on not stumbling over several slabs of concrete sidewalk heaved by roots of the big old maples. "Does your grandmother have many guests staying with her?"

"Not anymore, not since several motels opened around here."

They went up four steps to the wide, painted porch with a big wood-slat swing on the left and scattered comfortable-looking wooden rockers. Setting down the suitcase, he pulled open the screen door. "*Gra-am*, it's Keith. Someone's here to see you!"

"I'll be right down, dear." The voice sounded young and enthusiastic—not exactly what Andi expected of the woman she knew to be 75 years old.

He propped the door open with his knee and picked up the luggage, tilting his head to motion Andi in first. With the garment bag draped over her arm, she stepped inside the very large hallway as a slender, graying woman wearing denim shorts and a sleeveless knit top came running down the wide walnut staircase to greet her grandson with a hug and kiss.

He returned the embrace with no embarrassment. "Gram, this is Annie Marker, who has a problem. Annie, meet MaryJean McHenry, who's the probable solver of it."

They all started speaking at once, Keith explaining Andi's need for a place to stay, Gram "hoping to live up to expectations," and Andi, smiling at her own honesty in stating, "This does appear to be perfect."

"What a babble, all of us together!" Mrs. McHenry exclaimed. "But yes, I *can* help—if you find the accommodations satisfactory."

Refraining from saying that *anything* that made it

possible for her to stay here would be satisfactory, Andi simply nodded when invited to see the rooms.

They passed oversize doorways to two impressive rooms on either side of the downstairs hall—which itself could be an extra-large room in most houses. Even with massive pieces of excellent old furniture, there was much open space.

As the women started up, Keith offered, "Call if you decide to stay, Annie, and I'll bring your things."

Turning on the bottom step, she looked directly into his eyes. So, since she was five-eight, that would make him well over six feet. "I know you're in a hurry and I'm sure I'll like the room, so we can take them now." But then she almost wished that he wasn't right behind her, for he'd surely notice her slightly uneven gait.

He followed them up to the landing, then the six additional steps to another hallway as wide as the lower one. Here, also, were walnut or mahogany chests, a glass-fronted bookcase, and a huge, curve-topped armoire.

Mrs. McHenry crossed to the first room on the left, which had old-fashioned wallpaper delicately patterned with violet nosegays, trellises and ivy vines. The bed's high, carved headboard and the other furniture could have been museum pieces, and the well-worn oriental rug made Andi want to kick off her sandals and relax. "It's *beautiful*, Mrs. McHenry. I'll be more than comfortable here."

"Come see the other rooms. You might like one of them better."

They checked the even larger north front corner room. A quilt-covered white-iron daybed stood along one wall, in addition to furniture comparable to that in the first.

The large bathroom had obviously been constructed from unused space at the front of the hallway. Its white, claw-foot tub and pedestal washbowl were like some she'd seen in magazines, probably the same fixtures bought when the house was "modernized" eons ago with indoor plumbing.

"This will be yours to use—if you stay."

"I do want to."

"Well, look at this, too—The Violet Room." And she opened the door of the other front corner one. There was no need to ask why she'd called it that. Violets were rampant on the wallpaper; there was a violet pattern around the edge of the large carpet; violet-decorated bedspreads adorned both double beds; and there were even violet-patterned vases!

Keith drawled, "She sorta got carried away here."

Andi feared Mrs. McHenry might be offended, so was relieved to hear her chuckle. "I've always loved violets, so was delighted to find wallpaper for both rooms. But my birthday was right after the paper was hung, so, without checking, *everyone* gave gifts with violets." Her hand moved in a slow arc, palm upward. "Behold the results!"

Andi smiled. "Each room's lovely in its own way, but I think I'll choose the other violet room, with just one bed. Perhaps someone else will need these extra beds."

"Possible, not probable." Mrs. McHenry sounded as content as her shrug indicated. "Nowadays, it's mostly people from the hospital or a nursing home who call to see if out-of-towners can stay for a night or so.''

Back in "her" room, the suitcase was placed on the bed and the computer and attaché case on the smaller, marble-topped chest of drawers, while the garment bag was hung in the closet. Keith kissed his grandmother on the cheek, said, "'Bye for now," to Andi, and ran down the stairs.

Mrs. McHenry smiled. "That boy, he's always hurrying!"

"He mentioned having a date."

His grandmother cocked her head. "Oh?"

Chapter Two

Andi had been invited to come downstairs for some supper after she'd unpacked, so was soon following sounds of activity toward the rear of the downstairs hallway.

She passed a third, regular-size door on her left, and then was in the huge kitchen with built-in floor-to-twelve-foot-ceiling cherry cupboards. There was an old, galvanized sink and early-model refrigerator/freezer and electric stove—but also a top-of-the-line mixer, blender and microwave on the counter. "What a pleasant kitchen to work—to *live* in!"

"I especially like having all these windows on two sides—except when washing them." Her hostess took bowls from a cupboard and reached into a wooden drawer for soup spoons. Setting them on the table, she brought a container from the microwave and divided its contents. Andi also saw a basket of home-baked biscuits on the table. "I hope you like chicken-and-corn soup, Miss—*Miss?* Marker."

"Please...I'm Annie," she said, stumbling slightly over the almost-*Andi*. "And yes, I'm unmarried."

"Okay, Annie. And you call me MaryJean, if it doesn't bother you to say that to someone of my advanced years. Or just *Gram*, if you like."

Mrs. McHenry's attitude as she spoke of "advanced years" made it plain that she felt anything but elderly. Considering her reason for being here, Andi had no difficulty making her choice. "Since Keith called you 'Gram,' I'd prefer that."

"Fine." She motioned for Andi to sit near the corner, on the long side of the wooden extension table, while she took the matching cane-seated chair at the end. "This soup's a favorite of my family. I make huge batches, eat some, give some away, and put the rest in the freezer."

Andi's spoon moved among chunks of chicken, pieces of hard-boiled egg, tiny dumplings, and yellow kernels of corn in broth as she waited for Gram to take the first bite—

"Do you want to return thanks or shall I?"

Andi's spoon clunked against the side of her bowl as she hastily set it down. "Would *you*, please?"

Gram reached for Andi's hand and bowed her head. "We thank you, Lord, for your many blessings, including bringing Annie safely this far, even though she had car trouble."

Andi shifted uncomfortably as the prayer continued. "Help the boys be able to fix it, and help this delay to not interfere too much with her plans. I appreciate her being here, where I pray she'll find rest, peace and renewal."

How long has it been since I was prayed for? she

wondered. Mother used to pray with her at bedtime, and when just the two of them ate lunch or dinner together, they'd sometimes hold hands like this. Mother also took her to Sunday School and church, before all those trips to the hospital began.

Gram concluded. "...Thanks, also, for this nourishing food. Amen." She patted Andi's hand before reaching for her spoon. "Where are you heading? And when must you get there?"

Andi had expected her story to be easy to tell, but now, after that prayer, felt uncomfortable—even though convinced that her motives justified her actions. She *had* to learn about her family—about The Cousins.

"There's no set time—no exact destination," she admitted. "Just driving around New England and sightseeing, so I don't mind staying a while."

Gram's head was cocked to the side again, birdlike. "All by *yourself?* Won't you get lonely?"

Probably Gram would miss people. Surrounded by family as she was, she probably never had a chance to be lonely. "I wanted to spend time by myself." She surprised herself by adding, "I just lost an especially good friend."

She was embarrassed by tears in her eyes; they still came too readily. "It was—an automobile accident. Jon was killed."

Gram's hand was on her arm and then she was getting up from her chair to stand beside Andi's, drawing her close, holding her. "I'm sorry."

No sounds except for a truck's passing on the street. The buzzing of a fly at the back door. A distant lawn mower. Yet in some strange way Andi felt comforted.

Gram returned to her seat. "My Phil died suddenly, too. I know what a shock that is."

Andi looked into the clear blue eyes of this woman whom she was already beginning to consider a friend. "I'm sorry, too—about your loss."

They began eating and the on-and-off conversation concerned soup ingredients, and the size of the community and what went on in it. "Next weekend will be busier," Gram told her. "It's the annual Firemen's Carnival."

"What's that?"

"All the towns around here, except Dalton, have their own volunteer fire companies. We think Sylvan Falls's is the best—and it *is*. We win contests year after year. But it's horrendously expensive to buy equipment and pay for repairs and uniforms and stuff, so they need money-making projects.

"Over at Caldeer, they have hunters' breakfasts round-the-clock for three days at the beginning of deer season, and at Murrayville, there are elaborate skeet shoots a couple of times each year. At Parsons Springs, next north of here, they specialize in family-style dinners for Mother's Day and Thanksgiving and Easter—times like that. But here in Sylvan Falls and at a number of other places, there are carnivals."

"What is your carnival like?"

"Well-l-l, it's one week when everyone in the community has fun together. There are parades some nights—pet parades, floats and fire equipment and vehicles—that sort of thing. Our school band performs, as well as any from other towns that can be coerced into comin'. And the Little Leaguers, 4-H members, Scouts and kids from twirling and dance studios are here, even nursery schools—so there are *many* adults and children watching from the sidewalks.''

She got up, retrieved a half-gallon carton of butter pecan ice cream from the freezer, and scooped large servings into cereal bowls. ''The Firemen's Building and lot are one block back and two over that way,'' she said, flicking her hand in a southwesterly direction.

''A day or two before the official opening, trucks arrive with the Ferris wheel, merry-go-rounds, Spiders, Moonwalks, slides—all sorts of things. In the meantime, the firemen and the Auxiliary, which is *very* active, set up things for chicken barbecues or pig roasts or whatever dinners are to be served. Others prepare the pizza, ice cream, and hot dog and barbecue stands. Or whatever.''

She returned the carton to the freezer. ''By the time it's all done, hundreds are involved—baking cakes or pies, setting up tables, selling raffle tickets for a donated quilt, cooking for the dinners, overseeing a coin-toss booth where prizes are anything from stuffed bears to vases.''

''That sounds interesting. I almost wish I could stay.''

''Well—'' she placed Andi's dessert in front of her and returned to her own chair ''—maybe you can.''

Andi was grateful for that, but tried to keep from appearing too eager. ''Depending on the car...''

Andi hadn't realized how tired she was until she tried to watch a comedy on TV. She sat with Gram in the room to the left of the front door, which Gram referred to as the "TV room."

Gram seated herself in the center of the tapestry-covered couch and picked up her knitting. Andi chose the spindle-backed rocker with cushioned, petit point seat partly because it looked comfortable, but also to be facing the front windows looking onto the street.

She hoped others of Gram's family might come, but they didn't. She got up during a program break and walked over to the upright piano, where photos were displayed on its flat top. "Are these your children and grandchildren?"

Gram laid down her handwork and came over to pick up a framed picture. "This is our oldest, Phyllis, a second-shift nurse at the hospital, and her husband, Hal Bastian. He's a mechanic. Did you meet him at the garage?"

She shook her head. "I arrived late and saw no one except Keith, who came when he heard the buzzer."

"Well, they have only one child, Evelyn, and she teaches second grade. And this is her husband, Frank, and their kids, Brock and Melody—aged six and four."

The children were leaning like bookends against their seated parents—bright-eyed, dark-complexioned Melody, with an impish look on her face; blond Brock, more serious.

Andi indicated the children. "They're beautiful. Are they as different as they look?"

Gram laughed. "If they came in right now, Brock would sit with us and carry on a grown-up conversation, while Melody, the whirlwind, would be checking out the kitchen, running up and down the stairs—

and might very well be going through your things upstairs!''

"In that case, I'll keep things locked.'' She must do that, at least with her laptop. She didn't need inquisitive little hands revealing—or destroying—data!

Some pictures appeared to be recent shots and some, much older. Andi picked up one of a little boy, dressed in a striped T-shirt and blue jeans, who proudly held a disgruntled-looking calico cat. Although the boy looked to be only six or seven years old, his wide warm smile and sparkling eyes were unmistakable to Andi.

"Is that Keith?'' she asked Gram, already knowing the answer. What a dear little boy he seemed. Her heart felt a rush of warmth at this precious glimpse into his childhood.

"Yes, Keith and one of his many pets. All the strays in town seemed to follow that boy home. Zack used to joke about opening a petting farm.'' Gram laughed.

Gram took the picture from Andi and gazed down at the image with a loving expression. "Our Keith…I couldn't love him more if he was my own blood.''

"What do you mean, 'your own blood'?''

"Well, my son Zack isn't Keith's natural father. Keith's father died when the child was less than a year old. It was maybe two years later when Zack married Shelby and legally adopted him.''

While Gram set the photograph back on the piano, Andi felt such a moment of sadness for Keith, having lost his biological father at such a tender age. Then a flush of excitement followed. She and Keith weren't even distantly related. She need not feel any concern at all about her attraction to him.

Gram reached for another photo, showing a middle-aged couple and a stunningly beautiful blonde. "This is Brad—Bradley Eugene McHenry—married to Paula, a lawyer. And their daughter, Vanessa. Her degree's in computer science, but she works as secretary to the president of a computer technical support company."

Hmmmmm, she thought. Gram didn't mention Brad's profession. But she hadn't said what Frank did, either, so that's probably not significant. "With that background, Vanessa's probably invaluable to her boss."

"She calls herself a—an *executive* secretary."

"Is that here in Sylvan Falls?" There was no mention of such a business in her file.

Gram slowly, precisely, replaced the likeness. "In Dalton. She lives there now, so I don't see much of her."

Is that disapproval in her tone? Andi wondered. "You saw a great deal of her when she lived at home?"

"Not as much as I'd have liked."

The phone rang, and Gram went to the kitchen. She was talking into what she later referred to as her "walk-around" as she returned. "...There's a lady from Chicago spending the weekend here...No, waiting for her car to be fixed...Yes, everything's fine here. How 'bout you?...Keith stopped for a few minutes, and all seems well with him.... I'd *love* to, Karlyn, if you promise not to go to a lot of trouble... Great! See you in church. And thanks..."

Andi had returned to her rocker, and Gram laid the phone among the balls of yarn as she returned to the sofa. "That was Karlyn, Zack's daughter."

Zack? That must be what they call Isaac Mark Mc-Henry, Gram's younger son who owns the garage—Keith's dad.

"She lives on the other side of town, in one of those new houses. She's a sweet girl—tough, though, thank goodness! That ex-husband of hers got another woman pregnant, one of Karlyn's friends—or so she'd thought! Anyway, Karlyn divorced him and he married Danielle Catherman a month before their baby was born. At least Karlyn got the kids and the house and child support. And she teaches art in the elementary school."

MaryJean's such a willing source of information, Andi thought, that we wouldn't have needed that investigator!

They watched one more comedy before Andi, using the arms of the chair to push herself up, said, "I'm *bushed.* I think I'll soak in the tub, then go to bed."

"I'll bet you're tired, especially with your leg..."

Neither Andi nor Gram had mentioned her injuries until now. "It's better than it was, but does still bother me."

Gram's dark blue eyes showed concern. "What happened?"

"I—" Did she want to get into this? "—I mentioned my friend's being killed in an accident. I was in the car with Jon when it happened, though I don't remember much after the first few minutes. I...guess I knew he was dead, that there was nothing to do, yet

I kept trying to free myself—to reach him.'' The horror was still there. She lived it daily—and nightly.

''And then there was—nothing at all till I came to in the hospital. And learned he was gone...''

The stairs seemed longer than when she'd climbed them earlier, and as she plodded upward she asked herself why she was talking so much about that accident. Not only had she mentioned his death during the evening meal, but now again.

I must get hold of myself, she thought.

Mrs. McHenry had told her that the dresser along the outside wall was for her use, so she put underclothes, T-shirts, sweaters and shorts in the second drawer. Into the top one went several good pieces of costume jewelry, along with socks, belts and other small items.

She placed four top-of-the-book-list novels and her travel alarm on the bedside chest, and carried her flower-print pajamas and toiletries to the bathroom.

While water ran into the tub, Andi took off her clothes, then twisted her hair, fastening it up on top of her head. Holding onto the rim of the high tub, she stepped in and lay back against its comfortably sloped end. What luxury! Many changes had been made in modern plumbing, but nothing beat the big old-fashioned tubs!

She dried her hands on a fluffy white towel before picking up the *National Geographic* from the stand beside her. Finishing the first article, she went on to the second, after adding more hot water to the bath.

She was tempted to go on reading, but told herself that Gram might want to use the facilities. Reluctantly climbing out, she dried herself and got into the cotton PJs.

Perhaps hearing the bathroom door open, Mrs. Mc-Henry came into the hallway from the second room on the left. "What time will you be getting up in the morning, Annie?"

"I'm—not sure."

"I was asking because of breakfast."

"Oh." She'd momentarily forgotten the second part of bed-and-breakfast. "Whatever suits you is fine with me."

"Well, I always go to Sunday School and church...."

"What time are they?"

"Sunday School at 9:30, church at 10:45."

"Do you get dressed and ready before eating?"

"Usually. Almost *always* when folks are staying here."

"So what time should I be downstairs?"

"Is 8:15 too early?"

There was hopefulness in her voice. "Sounds fine."

Andi had started toward her room again when she heard Gram say, "I hope you won't mind, but Keith often comes for Sunday breakfast, then we walk to church together."

"That makes it nice for both of you."

"Yes, it does. Especially since his fiancée broke off their engagement last fall—and went off with some fellow she'd known less than two months! Keith and Sandy used to go to church and everywhere together... You're welcome to go with us," Gram invited. "We have an excellent pastor."

Andi had no intention of allowing herself to be coaxed, so was evasive. "We'll see in the morning." She stopped to look at titles on the spines of old volumes in the tall, glass-fronted bookcase next to her doorway, and Gram came to stand beside her. "Most of these were Mother's, some *her* mother's—and some my own additions." Opening the doors, her hand caressed the books.

Recognizing only a few of the authors, Andi randomly pulled out one book, *Daddy-Long-Legs*. "These covers are attractive—like this one, with its vine-surrounded heart and still-red roses. Modern publishers could take lessons."

She opened the book and read aloud. "By Jean Webster, With illustrations by the author and scenes from the photo-play, produced by the Mary Pickford Company starring Mary Pickford." Curious, she turned the page and was not surprised to find its copyright date was 1912.

Several pages were coming loose, so she handled the fragile volume with care, appreciating that the black-and-white photos were as clear and sharp as when published. "May I borrow this tonight? I often read myself to sleep." Always *have* to, actually, said an inner voice.

"Of course—that or anything. I read them when a girl, my kids did, then the *grandkids*. You might as well, too."

It felt good to be included with the family of this friendly, outgoing woman. Andi sighed with contentment as she climbed into the high old rope-bed and leaned back on pillows propped against the headboard.

The book had large margins, so she supposed she'd finish the whole thing before falling asleep.

But she drifted off at page sixty-three.

Laughter, teasing, wind blowing her hair. The squealing of wheels making sharp turns, the exhilarating high of speed.

Excitement turning into concern.

Reaching out, *Please, Jon, slow down.*

Laughing reassurance that he'd never had an accident.

Child running into the road.

Scream of brakes. Grinding protest of car's frame.

Massive tree.

Thunderous crash of metal. Of glass.

Folding back of metal, wrapping itself around Jon.

Around her.

Agony…!

Andi awoke, gasping for air, reaching for Jon—who was not there. Staring wide-eyed around the unfamiliar room, lighted only by moon-glow filtered through maple leaves.

Submerged in terror.

Oh, God! But she'd given up on God long ago—as He'd doubtless given up on her.

Chapter Three

The door was closed, so turning on the light wouldn't waken Mrs. McHenry. That helped some, and Andi started those slow, deep breaths that the therapist had recommended.

Her panic gradually lessened and Andi got out of bed to walk around the room, barefoot, looking at pictures on the wall. She forced herself to examine minute details, to concentrate on realities, on the substance of her surroundings.

It might help to get a drink of water—but she stopped, hand on the knob, then leaned back against the door. This was a bed-and-breakfast, but would it make the owner nervous to have someone walk around in the middle of the night?

And it *was* the middle—2:28. With many hours yet to get through! But—and this was the good part—she'd slept several hours, without pills! She'd been trying so hard to get off all that medication.

She looked at the worn volume beside her bed. It

wasn't boring, but was not terribly exciting, either—
not like the books she usually read. She'd brought
novels by top mystery writers, hoping they'd lure her
into a plot in which she could lose herself—yet it had
been the old-fashioned *Daddy-Long-Legs* that accomplished that.

She carried the book to the dainty little ladies'
rocker which, low and comfortable, seemed perfect
for this room, and read several more short chapters
before moving back to bed. Her leg bothered her, so
she rubbed that while continuing to find out more
about the orphan girl who was given a college education by an anonymous benefactor, and thus thrust
into an entirely different environment from that in the
foundling home where she'd spent her life.

The viewpoint character's reactions to people and
events are delightful, Andi thought, and her little
sketches add poignancy—but how little similarity
there is between her college experiences and mine!

She turned pages until, at 3:17, she heard the blast
of sirens and recalled Gram's speaking of the volunteer fire company. Before long, emergency vehicles
and equipment were rushing by on the previously
quiet street.

Going to one of the windows, she saw ladder
trucks, pumpers, an ambulance, and other equipment
she had no names for, all with flashing lights. She
hoped no one would get hurt and that the fire would
be extinguished quickly.

Eventually she became drowsy, put the book aside,
turned off the light…and slept.

Setting the alarm had seemed unnecessary when
getting ready for bed, but she had to hurry to get

downstairs by 8:13—three minutes before Keith came in the front door and sauntered through the hallway into the kitchen. He kissed Gram and greeted Andi, "Good *morning*. You look like you got a good rest."

"So do you," she responded. He'd been good-looking in coveralls, but was downright gorgeous with the white, short-sleeved cotton shirt emphasizing the musculature of his tanned arms. And the light-weight, gray, sharply creased slacks made those legs look even longer.

"I'm afraid that's another case of appearances being deceiving." He grinned before turning to Gram. "I was on that fire call last night, out at Alf Harner's place—the trailer he set up for his daughter, back of their house."

Andi started to say that she'd seen the vehicles go by, but he continued. "Nobody hurt, thank God, but a lot of damage. I don't know *why* Marjie was doing laundry at that time of night, but apparently lint in the gas dryer caught fire."

They talked more about that before Gram asked about last evening's date. Apparently amused, Keith glanced toward Andi, his brown eyes sparkling. "Everything went well, my dear grandmother. And how was *your* evening?"

Her response was just as breezy. "Very good. We watched TV and visited, and the time passed quickly."

Andi felt a bit uncomfortable about having shared that with Gram, so she changed the subject. "Do you live in town?"

"Sure do—down the street a block."

She didn't think that she should ask about a family,

but on this block the houses appeared to be too large and old for a single young man. She brought herself up short as she looked around the kitchen in this beautiful old home; some might think this too big for Gram, too, yet Andi couldn't imagine her living in a two- or three-room apartment.

"How are you coming with that staircase?" Gram asked.

"Slo-o-owly. Very slowly. But I am making progress, and that's what's important."

He'd been pouring orange juice as Gram turned the French toast in a heavy, cast-iron skillet. Instead of setting Andi's glass on the table, he handed it to her. "What are you doing with your...*staircase?*" she asked.

"Long before I bought the house at auction two years ago, some idiot painted all the wood in the house *white*—even the hand-turned spindles on the banisters, which are as elaborate as those in this house. I checked and found that everything's made of chestnut, if you can believe that!"

She was evidently supposed to be impressed. "I'm sorry, but I don't understand why that's special."

He carried maple syrup to the table, and sat down. "I don't know about Illinois, but one of the major deciduous trees in Pennsylvania used to be a very large one—the chestnut. Many houses and barns around here were built of its lumber, as was much of the furniture. But then a blight came along and wiped out the American chestnut—"

"All of them? Just like *that?*" She snapped her fingers.

"Just like that," he replied. "All of them."

Gram corrected him. "There are still a few, Keith...."

"Not like they were, though. What have survived are runty little things, more like large bushes which live long enough to have a few crops of small nuts, then die."

Gram placed the coffeepot on a trivet and joined them at the table. "Penn State's forestry department, and other specialists, are working on resistant strains, but I don't know how they're making out. But it would be generations before we see chestnut lumber suitable for construction."

"And so," her grandson went on, taking Gram's hand in his, "I want *my* chestnut exposed in all its glory."

Andi hadn't expected him to reach for her hand too, but willingly gave it, when he said, "Gram lets me offer the prayer when I come for breakfast."

That sounded fine until, looking deeply into her eyes, he suggested, "You may have that privilege if you'd like."

"Oh, no!" Startled, she would have withdrawn her hand had he not been holding it firmly. "Thanks, anyway."

This was the second time she'd been in this kitchen during prayers. Keith asked that those teaching and preaching would be blessed and that today's services would go well and be meaningful for all who participated.

And then, quite conversationally, he prayed for Andi—thanking God that "Annie" had gotten here safely in spite of car trouble, and asking that her car could be fixed without too much difficulty.

She sneaked a look at him when he asked that her leg would soon get completely well. She'd said nothing to him about the accident nor her leg, and doubted that Gram had.

It was while eating her second piece of French toast covered with syrup that Keith asked if she was joining them for church—and *she* realized she might like to. "Will your family be there?" That would be an additional incentive, she thought.

"Mom and Dad rarely miss. And my sister's always there with her two kids."

"How would I dress if I go with you?"

Gram's open face showed pleasure. "You look fine as you are, Annie, with that lacy blouse, slacks and sandals."

"Are pants okay?"

"Of course—though you have time to change into a skirt if you'd feel more comfortable."

She hadn't meant to glance toward Keith, but saw his nod. "I'm with Gram. You *do* look good, just as you are."

Heat crept up into her face, and totally unnecessary words spilled out. "I've been wearing pants most of the time since the accident—because of the scars...."

His glance flicked downward, then back to meet hers. "Are they really that bad?" he questioned softly.

"To me, they are."

His even, white teeth gnawed his lower lip. "Are you...a competent judge of that?"

That ankle and foot tucked behind the left one and were pulled as far back as they'd go under her chair. Her chin tilted upward. "I *am* the judge of that."

His gaze held hers for an uncomfortable moment before he looked toward Gram and asked her to pass the syrup.

Now I've blown it! she chastised herself. I shouldn't be so supersensitive. But they'd asked her to go with them, and she would.

It had been years since she'd been in church except for weddings and funerals. She used to go with Mother when they still lived in Claremont, back before Dad quit working for someone else so he could try developing his ideas and patents into practical inventions.

That was when Mother went back to teaching, so there'd be a steady income. Things were tough financially, and though she'd tried, Andi hardly remembered Dad from those days when he routinely spent twelve to eighteen hours a day at work.

But she'd never forget Mother—always cheerful and supportive, always there for Brownies, then Scouts, and for swimming and flute lessons. Never missing a band or choir concert. Taking her to the library and the museum.

By the time Dad had his twentieth patent; by the time the plant was built in Chicago and things were going really well *there,* Mother's health had begun to fail.

In spite of the cancer, she'd been able—at what cost to herself?—to furnish and decorate the new house and to serve as hostess for countless business dinners. When she went with Dad on trips to resort cities and other wonderful jaunts tied in with business, Andi was left at home. Mother would come back more exhausted than when she left, and gradually cut back on traveling. And on entertaining.

It had been fun having Mother around more, but Andi had not known the reason until six months before her death.

Why didn't you tell me, Mother? Andi silently wondered. Why didn't you let me know what you were going through? Oh, yes, I was busy with school and doing things with friends, but those weren't important. I'd much rather have spent that time with you....

They passed two churches—one stone, the other brick—as they walked to the vinyl-sided church on Maple and Second streets. Smaller than the others, it resembled those on Christmas cards: white, with a corner bell tower, and large old pin oak and maple trees along the front and side.

They entered the sanctuary through the red front door, Keith carrying a tall pottery vase filled with Gram's multicolored iris. Striding up the center aisle, between the rows of pews, he set the arrangement on a marble-topped table in front of the centrally placed pulpit.

He shook his head when Andi asked if the screening around the organ and choir, and the ornately carved pulpit and high-backed cushioned chairs on the platform, were made of chestnut. "I'm fairly sure they're walnut."

The sun shining through the stained-glass windows on her right gave an iridescent glow to everything, and she found herself whispering, "This is lovely."

"We like it." The wrinkles radiating outward from

the corners of Gram's eyes deepened, and her voice showed pleasure. "Maybe partly because the Mc-Henrys and the Barkers—*my* side of the family—have come here for generations. It's home."

How odd, thinking of church as "home," Andi thought.

"You have a choice," Gram said. "I'd like to take you with me, of course, but Keith's in the Builders' Class—mostly young adults. You'd probably like that best."

"That sounds like a good idea." But perhaps Keith wouldn't like that. Turning, she asked, "Is that all right?" Perhaps she was putting him in a bad situation, what with his date last night.

If he had reservations, he didn't express them. As they entered the hallway, he introduced her first to Patsy Harriman, the pastor's wife, then to others as they went down broad steps to the area beneath the sanctuary. Nine men and women were seated in a large circle, while others stood around a table holding a large metal urn and tray of cookies.

"Tea or coffee, Annie?" he asked, and she chose the former. She wasn't thirsty, but holding one of those foam cups would give her hands something to do. However, introduced as Gram's friend, she found that she need not have worried about being accepted.

Karlyn Tinsman, Keith's sister, was one of the last to arrive. It turned out that she was the teacher—a tall, outgoing, hazel-eyed woman in her mid-thirties, wearing her dark brown hair in a French twist.

She accepted being teased about her lateness—saying she'd lost track of time while preparing for a picnic—and proved to have a delightful sense of humor and an aptitude for getting input from students.

Even Andi contributed a thing or two—which she'd never have expected. Toward the end of this class on stewardship, Karlyn read something from the Bible about "talents," which Andi gathered didn't refer just to one's abilities or skills, but also to the use of financial resources in a way pleasing to God, as well as to others.

"Congratulations!" Karlyn was beaming as though she really meant it. "You have just won the sweepstakes and are receiving ten million dollars, coming to you in a lump sum. I'd like you to take the next few minutes to make a list of what you're going to do with your windfall."

Cheers and laughter greeted this announcement, and the man to Andi's right—Jeff-something—waved the blank sheet she'd just handed him. "Way to *go*, Karlyn, giving us paper from an extra-long legal pad!"

When someone complained about Uncle Sam getting *his* big cut first, Karlyn shrugged. "I'm feeling generous today. We'll make that ten million *after* taxes."

There were good-natured comments and joking, and Andi noted that most participants began doing what was requested. Several, however, seemed to have difficulty thinking of more than a couple of things, and one completely ignored the assignment.

If she really believed that God did this sort of thing, she'd wonder if He meant for her to be here this morning.

Keith, whose paper was being filled with remarkably neat writing, nudged her arm. "Come on, Annie, join in. Today you're one of us."

"I'm—not sure what to put down...."

"You must have had times when you thought, 'If I had enough money, I'd like to...whatever.' Well, here's your opportunity to spend a lot—quite painlessly."

She tried to suppress the smile she felt coming. *If you only knew, Cousin Keith—if you only knew!*

Well, she and Dad had decided on large endowments to universities, so she wrote: "Schools and Education." And "Red Cross" and "Salvation Army," because Dad had seen, long ago while he was a marine, how well they'd helped those in need.

"Grants for Cancer Research," because of Mother.

She'd just written, "Family and Friends," when Karlyn said, "Now put *1, 2,* and *3* by those you'd do first."

Keith was giving frowning attention to "Contributions," while Jeff was griping, "How does a guy prioritize taking his family on a round-the-world cruise or hiring the best golf pro in the world to improve his swing?"

A short, heavy man across the circle hooted, then assured Jeff that the latter would be a waste. "There's no *way* you'll ever get that swing of yours under control!"

Jeff stage-whispered, "Don't judge our whole church, Annie, on the nastiness of one man."

"I won't." She laughed. "I promise."

Keith had crossed out several numbers and was still putting others before entries, when Karlyn announced,

"Time's up! Now, please share your first three with us."

There was laughter and some groans, but no one volunteered. "Okay, how 'bout the first one?"

Andi was surprised that it was Jeff who led off with a serious response. "I suspect most of us would do what I'd want to—pay off all debts. In my case, that includes mortgage, car and loans for college expenses."

Some nodded, and he continued, as thoughtfully as before, "My second would be setting up trusts for the kids' education—and I'd investigate the possibility of locking in at least one fully paid tuition at Penn State."

"Very good! Anything else you'd like to share with us, Jeff?" When he shook his head, Karlyn asked, "And now, who's our next brave soul?"

A young red-haired woman said that since they lived in a too-small rented house, she'd first of all buy a place big enough for all of them, preferably with land. And since she and her husband had been wishing the kids could attend Dalton Christian Academy, she'd use some for that. Three children were presently in public school, and the youngest would begin kindergarten in the fall.

"What about you, Keith?" his sister enquired. "You've been busily writing."

"I still am. I'm not finished yet."

Jeff reached across Andi to grab Keith's almost-filled sheet, and held it up for all to see. "I can't even *write* that fast, much less think about what I should put down!"

Keith patiently held out his hand for it. "My num-

ber-one priority has to be giving a tithe to the Lord—
but I had trouble knowing in what form that should
be. Some of my other expenditures could come from
that million.''

"Like what?''

"Oh, things for the betterment of society or, under
certain conditions, of individuals. What about a new
pumper for the fire company, or gifts to a specific
department of the hospital, or to the Pregnancy Center
Project? Or perhaps to Habitat for Humanity? Should
they be part of *this* tenth, or would they be in separate
categories—perhaps numbers four, five, and seven?''

Several entered that discussion, and Andi paid avid
attention. Keith, having brought up the topic, continued to be involved with it, and helped Karlyn encourage those hesitant about expressing opinions.

Two others stated they'd written "Tithe" as their
first item, and Andi gathered that was the same as
"one-tenth.'' She knew that the many donations and
endowments made by her father or in the name of the
company would add up to more than that—and each
was carefully noted for tax purposes.

She fleetingly wondered what her university or
country club friends or co-workers would think of this
conversation. What might they say if they were here?

Was it possible any would agree with this consen-
sus? She doubted that, but it wasn't the sort of thing
they discussed. She couldn't even say how Jon
thought of money—*his* money. He *had* to have
thought about it, didn't he? Or had he just spent,
wanting to be liked, needing…what?

She'd had wonderful times with him, and they'd
talked of getting married—but she now faced the fact

that during these last years she knew little of what went on inside. She'd tried to bring up deeper issues, but he'd quickly turn her away from them, sticking to fun things.

Had he been hiding from her? From himself?

She pulled herself back to the present. She shouldn't be dwelling on this now, especially *here*.

Karlyn was tying things up. "...What's important to *you*—important enough to top your list of ways to spend money? And what do you consider really worthy of your time? There are necessary things like sleeping, eating, doing essential shopping, and spending 40 hours at work for many of us, and/or with baby and child care for some.

"But we still have—though I know it often doesn't seem like it—hours or minutes when we're not required to do specific things. What about those? What *are* you doing with your free time?

"And how well are you controlling your thoughts? It's true that anything can enter your mind, but what priorities have you set as to which ones remain, permitting them to take over? Just happy ones? Unhappy ones? Family-related? Service-oriented? Totally self-serving?"

She'd been at the chalkboard for the last few minutes, but now returned to her chair, part of the circle again. "We often don't even try to control what we're thinking. And thank God—literally!—that nobody knows what those thoughts are. Wouldn't that be embarrassing?"

Andi's glance circled the group as she wondered how many had secrets that they, like she, wouldn't want anyone else to know. Probably everyone.

"We often forget that God knows every one of our thoughts. These precede our moods, words and dealings with others—*including* what we do with what we have!"

Her eyes met those of each person. "It's easier to consider how to spend money when you still have nine million or more left—but you do, right now, have money. So...what *will* you do with your paycheck or other sources of income?

"And you do have your life. What will you do with that? Settle for self-gratification or momentary pleasures? Or do you want it to count for something more...? Those are your decisions."

Andi just sat there, not paying attention to the closing prayer, not really hearing it. What do I want from my life? she thought. From our money?

She had many questions; she did not know if they'd ever be answered.

Chapter Four

Gram was waiting at the top of the steps, then led the way into the sanctuary, which looked different with perhaps a hundred brightly clad people in the pews. Andi felt conspicuous coming into the front of the large, sunlit room, but followed as Gram started back the outside aisle.

Smiling and nodding to friends, Gram led the way into the empty fifth pew, to sit along the center aisle. Andi had stepped back to allow Keith to precede her if he chose, but his hand on her elbow indicated that she should go first.

She wondered again about last night's date. Might his having a not-too-unattractive, auburn-haired woman sitting by him in Sunday School and church cause resentment?

Gram got her attention. "That blonde—the third one coming into the front row of the choir—she's Zack's wife. Keith's mother. A soprano..."

Andi smiled and nodded, but with the organ play-

ing and choir sitting down, each member with head
bowed, it seemed inappropriate to respond verbally.

"You'll meet her at Karlyn's—she did mention
she'd like you to come to the picnic, didn't she?"

Andi whispered, "Karlyn invited me after class."

There was the call to worship. The singing of a
hymn, which sounded familiar. Scripture reading and
prayer. An outstanding, joyful choir anthem. Taking
up an offering—and she had no idea how much to
put in. Checks sent to charities were large, but
here…?

Those beside her were holding envelopes something like Mother had used, so that gave no clue. She
withdrew a ten-dollar bill from her wallet, folded it
in half, then over again, and placed it, number side
down, in the deep, highly polished wooden collection
plate. As she passed it on, she noted bills of various
denominations among the envelopes, so assumed
she'd done all right.

The pastor, probably under forty, seemed comfortable conducting the service, and his sermon was well
organized and interesting—though Andi's attention
was often on those around her.

Was Keith's father here? She wished there had
been pictures to go with the detective's information.

And that reminded her to take her camera along.
Candid shots shouldn't raise suspicion, and she'd like
to show them to Dad. And she'd probably want to
look at them, also, after returning.

Andi had shared Gram's hymnal for the two songs
before the sermon, but Keith held his toward her for
the last one. As she reached to hold it, her forefinger

touched his. Did he notice that? Or hers quickly drawing away?

He was an excellent baritone, and she found herself smiling up at him as she shifted from melody to alto. As the organist put in extra notes between the last two verses, he whispered, "You have a lovely voice, Miss Marker."

And she whispered back, "So do *you*, Mr. Mc-Henry," then wondered if people noticed their grinning at one another.

Gram knew everyone, and seemed to feel Andi should meet them, but it was Keith who introduced her to his parents, both of whom appeared friendly and outgoing.

"We'll see you at Karlyn's," Shelby said. "I must get home and pick up the salad and cake—and get into casual clothes." She turned back to add, "Be sure to bring your swimsuit, Annie. It's been warm enough that the water in the pool's quite comfortable."

"I—didn't expect to swim, so didn't bring one."

"Don't worry. I have extras." And she was gone.

Andi looked after her, wishing she'd said not to bother. Oh, well, that didn't matter—until she noticed Keith looking at her strangely, and wondered if he might be remembering her statement about usually wearing pants.

Back in her room, she hung her lightweight linen pants in the closet and took out a brightly colored sundress. It was long and full enough that the scars would remain hidden even when she was seated.

Keith had said he'd see Gram and her shortly, and she wondered if he might be going to pick up his date.

I hope he does, she told herself. That would get her over this wondering, this silliness, this....

No acceptable word came to mind as she leaned closer to the mirror to apply lipstick. But when she looked into the blue eyes in the mirror, she noted that the slight smile on her lips had failed to reach them.

Replacing the tube's cap, she stifled a sigh. Rule number one, Miss Annie Marker, or whoever you are: Thou shalt not fall in love. Which was fine to say— but why did she even consider that warning?

Why should that word, *love,* have even entered her mind?

She was in the kitchen when Keith entered by way of the back door. "All ready?"

"I think so," Gram said, "but it doesn't *feel* right."

"Why is that?"

"Karlyn made me promise not to bring more than one dish, so that's the macaroni salad there."

"You're a literalist if I ever saw one. You cover the top with a whole bottle of stuffed green olives and a can of big, ripe ones, so you're *still* bringing several foods, though they're now in one dish!"

"Well—" tossing her head "—the kids like olives!"

"Yes, we *do!*" He popped the black one from the very center into his mouth. "So let's go, ladies. My car's blocking the alley."

Andi opened the back door on the driver's side as he assisted Gram into the front one. "Let me fasten the seat belt," he said and drew it across. "You care for the salad."

"And the olives," Gram murmured.

"And the olives."

They tried to include Andi in their conversation, but she didn't identify the man about whom they were speaking—someone scheduled for a brain scan. They'd driven through town and out past the high school when Gram pointed. "That big stone house on the right is Karlyn's. It was at the edge of town when they built it—before Joe Mueller died and his kids sold the farm to a developer!"

Andi wondered at the disapproval in her tone, but Keith reminded, "That was their right, Gram."

"But Jake always had a *fit* about this sort of thing!"

"Not enough to make him put that stipulation in his will, however..."

Andi was brought back again to the major reason that she was here. In addition to getting to know her relatives, she must make sure that decisions concerning Dad's will, and her own, cover as many bases as possible.

"Those cars nearer the garage won't be able to get out, dear," Gram murmured as Keith backed into the driveway.

He turned off the ignition. "But the road's narrow through here, and I prefer not parking along its side. I'll move mine if anyone wants to leave early."

They were instantly surrounded by four excited children, introduced to her as Evelyn's Brock and Melody, and Karlyn's Jake and—*Traci?*

Uh-oh, that investigator had made at least a couple of slipups. *Jake* was undoubtedly a nickname for the "John" he'd reported, but he must have heard the name of the beautiful, dark-haired five-year-old and assumed her to be a boy, *Tracy!* She'd watch more carefully for other errors.

Karlyn had come to the corner of the house to invite them to the backyard, and Keith was escorted, *tugged,* by Brock and Jake. Gram, handing Andi the salad, was "helped" by Melody and Traci.

Keith's parents were already there, Shelby giving Andi a special smile. "We're so glad you joined us! Mom's probably told you we have quite a few family get-togethers, and there's always room for friends."

Zack—tall, burly and middle-aged—strode over to take Andi's hand. "I understand we let you down yesterday."

"Nothing to feel sorry about, Mr. McHenry," she reassured. "I'm enjoying my stay in Sylvan Falls."

"Great!" His other hand clasped her shoulder. "It's a wonderful place to live, and it's good to hear that you appreciate it. If you'd like to stay indefinitely, we can keep putting off work on your car." He waggled his eyebrows the way Dad sometimes did.

This can't be genetic, can it? she wondered. But such a simple thing put her at ease. "Did your mother tell you I may stick around for a while?"

He grinned. "You'll find that in our family, *good* news gets passed around real quick."

She was glad that he stressed the word, implying they didn't gossip in negative ways. "She told me about the carnival at the end of the week."

His shoulders slumped and hands dropped to his sides. His words—"Don't remind me of that!"—

could have indicated despair, had his eyes not been bright with excitement.

"What's your part in all this?"

"Well, for starters, we have floats to finish."

"Floats? *Plural?*"

"Yep. Anyone can enter—churches, organizations, businesses. I happen to be active in First Church and in Rotary, *and* have a business."

"You don't need to help with all of them, do you?"

His wife responded to that. "For your own well-being, Annie, don't even *suggest* he not work on all of them!"

Shelby was obviously teasing, so Andi felt safe asking, "Isn't there something like conflict of interest involved here? I presume there's some prize involved."

Zack admitted, "They gave me a hard time about that when the garage won *once,* six years ago. But the church has received first prize—all of twenty-five dollars, incidentally!—six or eight times, and Rotary at least that often."

"Congratulations!" Her head tipped forward in a nod of approbation. "So what's the theme for yours this year?"

"Ah-ha! That's what they all ask." Again the active eyebrows. "But you have to wait like everyone else."

Phyllis Bastian, Gram's eldest offspring, was carrying food from the house to the long picnic tables, while Hal, her husband, turned hamburgers and hot dogs on the gas grill. "Hi, Annie." He was waving long-handled tongs high in the air, and she recalled that he was a mechanic at Zack's dealership. "I hear Keith made an unfortunate decision about your car yesterday."

Keith didn't look at all apologetic. "Once in a while I do make a decision."

"...And now that I see what a knock-out you are, Annie," he declared, "I see *why* he didn't come ask for advice."

"What can I say?" Keith looked at her with a crooked smile as he was dragged off by Brock and Jake for some game involving a beach ball.

Phyllis, whom Andi knew to be a second-shift supervisor of nursing at the community hospital, introduced her daughter, Evelyn Pinchot, as mother of Brock and Melody. They had little chance to visit, however, as the children soon came running to ask about putting on swimwear.

"Is Uncle Keith going in with you?"

Her daughter was bouncing up and down on tiptoe. "Can we, Mama? Can we go in swimming? He'll watch us."

"Is he putting on a suit and going *in* with you?"

The little girl's lower lip pushed out in a pout, and it was Brock who turned to beg Keith, who had followed them. He rumpled the six-year-old's hair. "Not now, kids. Look at that platter of hamburgers and hot dogs and the rest of the spread! There's no *way* I'm about to miss that!"

"Well, how 'bout later? Will you go then?"

"We'll see."

They ran to check the last of the meat, being piled on top of the others by their grandfather. Their mother stood there, shaking her head. "I never thought you'd get away with such an evasive answer, Keith."

"I can't believe it either."

Karlyn steered all four of the little ones toward the "wash-up station," beside the house, stocked with a supply of towels. Evelyn followed, murmuring, "It's simpler to *prevent* squirting one another with liquid soap than to give comfort after it's in their eyes."

Watching his sister with the children, Keith commented, "Karlyn's a very good mother, and also an excellent second-grade elementary school teacher."

Andi nodded, then asked, "Is everyone here?" She knew that Gram's son, Bradley, had not arrived with his wife—nor had their daughter, who lived in Dalton.

"Aunt Paula doesn't make it to many of our gatherings, but Vanessa usually does." They were walking toward the laden table. "Will Uncle Brad be here, Gram?"

"I'm—not sure. Paula's in the middle of that big defense case, you know. And Brad…is between jobs again."

Keith's lips tightened. "Oh."

Oh?

"I called Vanessa—left a message on her answering machine. Unfortunately, I seldom get through to her."

Andi wondered whether Gram's disappointment about "getting through" to this granddaughter had to do only with the impersonality of equipment.

The long table, covered with red-and-white checked paper and with matching red tableware, was filled with meats, salads, rolls, vegetables, casseroles, relishes and beverages. Karlyn was the only one not seated when she announced, "Last chance, everyone. Look around. If things aren't reported as missing, they won't be forthcoming."

Andi's laughter joined that of Keith and the others. Then Karlyn was offering a prayer of thankfulness before everyone began talking at once and starting dishes of food around the table. Plates were loaded. "No, Melody, you *can't* eat just pickles and chips," Andi heard the child's mother remind her.

A frankfurter fell off the platter as it got to Melody. "Yes, you may call the dog," Karlyn said.

A second hot dog got dislocated at Karlyn son's place. "Really? Another accident? Well, we'll just put it up here on the table till the picnic's over," his mom said.

Andi, an only child, was enchanted by the teasing, the joking, the good-humored give-and-take, the sharing of memories—and just plain *love* evident around this table. She answered when people spoke directly to her, but was content to listen and observe, her gaze moving from person to person and ears catching not only words but nuances as she stored memories.

The food was delicious, but this whole experience even more wonderful.

Everyone was so stuffed later that it was decided to postpone pie and homemade ice cream until later. The remaining food was carried back to the kitchen, where the *big* job was finding and filling smaller containers for leftovers.

But Andi wasn't part of that for long, as Brock and Jake coerced her and Keith into playing a game of croquet. "I've only done this twice in my life," she admitted, "so you must promise not to be too hard on me."

Jake informed them, "Brock plays better than I do, so *he* should be her partner. And I'll play with Uncle Keith."

Keith put a stop to protests from Brock. "Hey, guys, you asked Miss Marker to play, and now act like this? How would you feel if no one wanted to be *your* partner?"

Jake tried to bluster his way out, but Brock came to her. "I'm—sorry. I didn't mean to make you feel bad."

She had an almost overwhelming desire to throw her arms around him, to hug him close. "It's all right, Brock."

The six-year-old looked suspiciously close to tears. "I *hate* being left out!"

Never having been around young children much, she glanced up at the tall man beside her, needing guidance. Keith gave the tiniest of nods, which encouraged her to say, "*Nobody* grows up enough to not get hurt feelings sometimes, but I'm okay now."

She didn't look at Jake until he took a step closer and offered. "I'll be partners with you if you want me to."

Leaning over, she spread her arms to hug both of them. Looking up over their heads, she said to Keith, "I can play *golf*. Could that help at croquet?"

"I sorta doubt it. And to the best of my knowledge, the government hasn't got around to using their multimillion-dollar grants to check out this extremely important matter."

He looked and sounded so serious that the boys

didn't recognize this as humor, and Andi felt unexpectedly warmed at this interplay between him and her.

They decided against playing as couples; each would be on his own. This was accomplished with such laughter and enthusiasm that other family members gravitated to the lower, level portion of the property to cheer them on.

She was still trying to maneuver back through the middle wicket when Brock's ball hit the finish stake, followed shortly by Keith's. And she was delighted when Jake's then made it on his second turn. Picking hers up, she carried it back to them. "You guys are wonderful!"

She'd half expected to play another game, but they were eager to swim. Evelyn produced suits and towels for Brock and Melody, who ran inside with their cousins to change. Shelby was beside Andi as they walked back up the gentle slope. "I brought a dark blue tank suit and a multicolored maillot, so you take your pick."

I'd like to graciously refuse, she thought, even though I used to love showing off how good I look in swimwear. However, I'm here to learn about my family, not to be rude.

Accepting them with thanks, she went with her hostess into the huge stone house that looked as though it had been there for centuries instead of... "How long have you lived here, Karlyn?" she asked, after complimenting her on how perfect everything was.

"Nearly nine years. My ex-husband is co-owner, along with his father, of a large building supply company on this side of Dalton. They were just beginning their expansion into the construction business, as well—so our dream house was one of their first projects. Planned as a showpiece.''

"I love the spaciousness, the *openness* you've achieved. And all these windows!'' Andi's home in Chicago, built of huge sandstone blocks for some cattle dealer in the late 1800s, was almost castle-like with its many high-ceilinged rooms, but was darker inside than this house.

"My attorney fought hard to save this. It's a lot of house for just the kids and me, but I couldn't give it up.''

Karlyn put on a blue princess-style suit, while Andi changed into the maillot, and they walked together out the side door onto a wooden deck and down the steps to the large in-ground pool. The four children were joyfully and loudly enjoying the water. And Keith, at the far end, looked fabulous in white swim trunks.

But Andi's stomach tightened. She wasn't only seeing *his* long, tanned legs and torso; there was a striking blonde sitting beside him on the wood-crafted settee!

"Ahhh,'' Karlyn murmured. "Vanessa did come.''

Andi should have recognized from Gram's pictures that the tall, slim, golden-skinned woman was Brad and Paula's only child. Walking toward them, Andi was even more conscious than usual of those ugly still-red scars on her leg and thigh. Some day she'd check with a plastic surgeon, but wasn't yet ready to face another operation.

Karlyn continued, "...I'm glad she's here. We don't see enough of her anymore."

"Oh? Is there...some reason for that?" She told herself somewhat defensively that she was *supposed* to find out about everyone.

There seemed a moment of hesitation. "Vanessa knows she's always welcome. And she really is a nice girl."

Andi wondered at Karlyn's feeling that it was necessary to add that last sentence. "She's one of the most beautiful women I've seen in real life."

"Yes. She is."

The children were shouting for their croquet-friend to join them in the blue-and-white ceramic-tiled pool, but Karlyn told them, "Give her a couple of minutes. You don't get to have Annie *all* the time, you know. I want to introduce her to Vanessa now."

Pleased that they wanted to include her, Andi assured them that she'd soon be back. Is this what I've missed by being an only child? she thought. With no relatives around, beyond my parents?

Vanessa laid a long-fingered hand on Keith's knee, called attention to the approaching women, then leaned back in her seat. Her slightly husky voice sounded warm in greeting. "Hello. You must be Annie."

"Yes, she is," Karlyn acknowledged. "Annie, this is our cousin, Vanessa McHenry."

Andi took the several steps to offer her hand. "I've been looking forward to meeting you. I saw your picture on your grandmother's piano last evening. Your hair was a little longer, but otherwise you haven't changed at all."

Vanessa's glance flicked toward Keith, then back to Andi. "That was at least six years ago. Thanks for saying I haven't changed."

Keith drawled, "That's one thing about us Mc-Henry's—we age gracefully. Look at Gram over there."

Karlyn and Vanessa agreed, but Andi wondered if perhaps Keith had deliberately changed the conversation's focus. Gram was apparently considered a safe subject.

Chapter Five

Jake and Brock climbed from the pool, grabbed Andi's hands, and pulled her toward the water, reminding everyone it was *their* turn now.

"Let me get my sandals off," she pleaded as she reached the edge.

Then she smiled over her shoulder at Keith's announcement. "Enjoy her while you can. We all get chances."

Jake looked pouty, then brightened. "Uncle Keith, you can come in with us, too. We'd like that."

Yes, we would! she agreed silently. She was disappointed that he didn't regard her smile as an invitation—or didn't respond to it, anyway. She was an excellent swimmer and found her injured leg not much of a handicap. Besides, her physical therapist had suggested she spend more time in a pool.

After an enthusiastic game of swim-tag, touching each of the children in turn, she called for a personal time-out and climbed the poolside ladder. "I haven't been swimming much recently, and I'm older than you. I need to rest.''

She walked over to a bench which, being white, wasn't too sun-heated to lie upon. She looked around for Keith and saw him sitting with Vanessa, a short distance away. They seemed involved in a serious conversation. Vanessa looked upset and Keith's expression was sympathetic. Andi wondered what they were talking about, then realized it was none of her business.

A thought, at first dismissed, came back: were they romantically involved? Could Vanessa be his "unbreakable" date? Since Keith was Zack's adopted son, he was not a blood relation to Vanessa. Yet, something told Andi their relationship wasn't romantic. Or was that her own wishful thinking, she wondered.

Andi got to her feet, not wanting to look as if she was trying to eavesdrop. Zack was in the pool, playing a game with floating hoops—he and granddaughter Traci teamed against the other three. Andi walked past to join Phyllis. "Your Brock and Melody are delightful."

"Being their grandmother, I'm prejudiced, but do agree. They're interested in everything and everybody, and don't have a shy bone in their bodies!"

"Do you get to see much of them?"

"Not enough, except on my days off and during vacations. As a second-shift nursing supervisor at Dalton General, I'm usually not around after school."

"Do you enjoy your work?"

"Most of the time—though not as much as I used to.''

"Why is that?"

A shrug. "With all the new legislation, hospital mergers, HMOs, and changes in insurance, most challenging cases are immediately shipped out to a bigger hospital."

"Because it's better for the patients?"

"In our case, I'd categorically say that is *not* the case. We've always had an excellent staff, and I'd put our nursing care, lab work and doctors up against anyone's."

Andi learned their home was an old farmhouse about two miles toward Dalton. "It's on fifteen acres we bought about eight years ago. And we'll probably still be working at changes and improvements twenty years from now!"

Gram came to sit with them. "If you stay a while, Annie, maybe we can go out there one of these days."

"I'd like that." What an understatement! she thought. Just then Andi saw Keith jump off the side of the pool, deliberately making as big a splash as possible. Cries and squeals came from the children, but there was no doubt that they were delighted by his joining them.

"Everyone adores that man," Gram commented. "No matter how young or old they are."

Andi supposed that she should respond. "It did appear that way at church."

Phyllis laughed. "All the little old ladies vying for his attention?"

"And the teens," Gram agreed. "And the little ones."

Phyllis patted the seat beside her as her husband,

still dripping from the pool, joined them. "I can't figure what Keith does that draws everyone."

Hal sat down beside her. "If someone determines that and wants to bottle it, I'll volunteer for product testing." He gave Andi an obvious wink, earning him an equally obvious poke from his wife's elbow.

Vanessa joined them for a few minutes, before saying she must be back to Dalton in—glancing at her diamond-studded watch—less than a half hour. Karlyn walked with her around the house, coming back almost immediately. Andi heard diminishing sounds of a well-tuned automobile engine.

People were already speaking of other things. Hal asked where Andi was from and what she did for a living, but no one seemed overly familiar with Michigan State University or Chicago, for which she was thankful. And they had no reason to be curious about the computer company of which she implied she was an employee.

The lazy conversation varied from plans for the summer to the health of mutual friends to the state of government in Washington and Harrisburg. Evelyn mentioned the lack of support teachers get from parents and administration—and about the "correction" she'd recently been given for hugging a little girl who'd fallen on the playground. "And the books we're required to use for my second-graders! It's not "politically correct" for me to teach phonics here, so one of these days I'll undoubtedly be called on the carpet."

Phyllis looked alarmed. "Maybe you'd better not do it."

Evelyn laid a calming hand on her shoulder. "The

children *are* getting what's in the books—learning to differentiate words by seeing them over and over. In addition, however, I'm making sure my little ones learn the phonetic value of letters, letter groups and syllables, so they can sound out unfamiliar words.''

"I'm proud of you, Evelyn." MaryJean was beaming. "I remember your Brock and Melody reading storybooks to me long before they even started school."

"Part of that could have been memorization, from my reading to them each night, plus off and on during the day. Some of those books literally fell apart."

"I know. I did that for your mother and uncles—and never begrudged one second of it."

Phyllis nodded. "I have wonderful memories of our being propped against the headboard of my bed—or of one of the boys' beds—whoever's turn it was—while you read to us."

"One book of your choice for each of you."

"Even when I was old enough to read chapter books—which weren't called that back then—I always wanted to be included in your reading sessions."

"And how you griped when I insisted that one or two of your chapters were equivalent to a whole book chosen by Zack or Brad!"

Hmmmm, Andi thought. Zack before Brad, even though Brad's the middle child. Perhaps that's because he's not here today. I wonder why he isn't. Nor his wife. His daughter was, but left soon, and most of her time was spent with Keith.

"I want you to know I've experienced payback for all that crying of 'unfairness' I put you through,"

Phyllis was saying. "My nurses aren't always pleased with my scheduling of hours and vacation times, even though I try hard."

Her husband's palm moved affectionately up along her arm and shoulder, though his words to the others were made to sound like an appeal for sympathy. "If only she'd try that hard to be fair with *me*."

Keith had joined them. "Sorry, Hal, this isn't the group to come to for pity where *she's* concerned."

Hal stretched to kiss his wife's smiling lips, not needing to say anything more.

Keith stated that he must leave shortly, and asked his grandmother and Andi if they wanted to stay, or if he should take them home. Gram looked with raised brows at Andi, who shrugged. "That's up to you."

There were immediate offers of transportation, and Keith started his apparently usual round of goodbye kisses for Gram, his mother, Phyllis and Evelyn. Karlyn hurried down the steps from the house, and he reached for her. "You are just in time to receive an especially big hug and kiss, along with heartfelt thanks for hostessing us all. Again!"

She put her arms around his neck to say something Andi couldn't hear. His reply, though low, sounded like, "It will work out all right—at least I pray it will."

Hmmmm. What was that about? Andi hoped he wasn't aware of the increased heat in her cheeks when, a little later, he placed his hand on her arm. "For a moment there, Annie, I was tempted to forget you aren't a relative, too."

And she wondered if, had he not turned and left, she could have kept him from seeing her blush.

* * *

Things weren't the same without him. Oh, the four-acre lawn was just as lovely, the pool as warm, the people as friendly, and the leftovers for supper as delicious, but nothing, including another croquet match, was as much fun.

She continued trying unobtrusively to learn as much as possible about each person there, but was ready to leave when Evelyn, while saying her goodbyes, offered to drop them off on her way home.

A short time after their return, Gram answered when the phone rang—and handed it to Andi. She sank down into her rocker as the voice—*his* voice—said, "It's Keith. I hope you don't mind my calling."

Was that a question? "This gives me the opportunity to thank you for driving us to Karlyn's."

"You're welcome."

"Her children are delightful."

"Yes, they are—and she deserves them. Karlyn's a wonderful mother. And teacher. And person."

This isn't what he's calling about, thought Andi, but he'll have to be the one to change the subject. "I'm sure she is. And she has such a glowing personality."

"I—was hoping to have more time to visit with you."

He was the one who stayed with Vanessa so much of the time—and left early, she thought. "That could have been interesting."

"Look, Annie—" he seemed less at ease on the phone "—are you planning to leave as soon as your car's fixed?"

"Not—right away."

"Good." And it did sound as though he meant that. "Then I don't have to persuade Dad to *not* repair it."

She laughed. "Now I won't know which of you to blame if they say they don't have time to take care of it."

Keith chuckled. "I promise not to ask that of him if you'll agree to join me for dinner tomorrow."

"That sounds like a good deal." A *great* one, actually, she added silently. "What time would that be?"

"Perhaps a little before eight?"

"That should be fine. But Keith, where will we go? What should I wear?"

"There's an excellent steak house eight miles south of us. Or we can go to Dalton for Chinese or Indian food—or for a ritzy dinner at the Susquehannock Hotel."

"Which do you prefer?"

"That depends on who I'm with or what the occasion is, or where I haven't been for a while—all sorts of factors."

She kept her tone light. "In that case, I should insist on your making the choice."

"Well, then it will be somewhere informal. I'd like to get to know you better." There was a slight pause. "You seem to have a certain air of mystery about you."

"We met just yesterday, Keith." Gram's head was tilted forward as though full attention was required on the cross-stitching she was doing, but Andi knew she was listening. "I'd have to be exceedingly shallow for you to learn everything about me in this short a time."

"Point well-taken, Annie. And I expect to continue liking what I discover."

And I like what I've learned, too, she wanted to say. But she simply responded, "Thank you," before returning to the discussion of where they'd eat.

Her choice for reading tonight was another of Gram's old books, *Aikenside,* by Mary J. Holmes. The copyright page was missing, but Andi decided it must be at least as old as *Daddy-Long-Legs.*

After her shower, she again propped pillows against the headboard. She'd have to be careful how she handled this volume, too, since the back was starting to come off and there were several loose pages.

There was satisfaction in holding these books—a continuity, a special relationship between her and the original owner, who could have been born in the nineteenth century. And what of those since? Would MaryJean McHenry have been the second generation—or possibly third? Had girls from each generation read it, right down to today?

She'd never had any appreciation of Dad's stopping at used-book stores to browse. She'd even teased him about buying raggedy volumes with little monetary value, when he could afford any new book he could possibly want.

She began reading. The style was different from what she was used to—more flowery, with more of the author showing through. But it was interesting enough that she had every expectation of reading for an hour or two.

But it was less than thirty minutes later when she turned off the light.

* * *

She was amazed to see sunlight brightening the leaves outside her north-facing windows. How long had it been since she'd slept through an entire night? That would be even before Jon's death, when she'd worried that he wasn't yet ready to settle down—that maybe *she* wasn't ready to be married to someone who refused to take life seriously.

Yet she enjoyed being with him. And she thought she loved him.

Andi looked at her travel alarm, then checked the still-unfamiliar inexpensive watch on her wrist: 6:42! Morning. With no sleeping pills or tranquilizers. With no nightmares.

Arms above her head, she stretched until her toes just touched the foot of the bed. She'd almost forgotten how much shorter people were, back when these rope beds were made.

She reached toward the book placed beside the clock last night, fingertips gently caressing the reddish cotton cover and outlining the picture of a girl in a long skirt. She did not open it, however; she'd save it for tonight.

It was usually difficult to get up in the morning because of lack of sleep, or perhaps from lingering effects of medication. Today she did not get out of bed right away, either, but because it felt so good to just lie here enjoying the morning after a good night's sleep.

What would she do today? Could she help Gram? Perhaps get something from the grocery or pharmacy?

She was sure that Zack or Hal or one of the others would discover what was wrong with her car, but Dad's mechanic had assured her that nobody would have reason to suspect that she'd "fiddled with the engine."

Perhaps she'd have them give it a thorough inspection while they had it, though everything should be in tip-top condition. She might ask them to do some bodywork, since there was a dent in one fender and several small scrapes.

Andi smiled, remembering her "date" tonight—actually dinner with Keith—and she'd better remember it was nothing more than that. After all, they'd just met in the late afternoon of the day before yesterday. And even if he wasn't actually her cousin, he was one of the people she'd come to investigate.

She didn't like the way her mind phrased that; *investigate* had too negative a connotation.

Getting to her feet, she made the bed with the light chenille bedspread before going to the bathroom to get ready for the day. She tried to be quiet, but when she returned to the hallway she saw Gram's door open. After changing into a sleeveless knit top, lightweight pants and sandals, she went downstairs.

She meandered out to the kitchen and saw through a back window that Gram was pulling weeds from a pansy bed. Andi pushed open the screen door and went out onto the big crosscut round of wood that served as a step. "Good morning, Gram. Isn't this a beautiful day?"

"It certainly is!"

She looked as though about to rise, so Andi started down the brick walk. "Can I help with something? It's too lovely to stay indoors."

"You can stay and talk with me," Gram invited.

"I don't often have anyone to visit with while gardening."

"Have you always planted so many flowers?"

"Oh, goodness, no! When the kids were still at home, this whole side of the yard was filled with vegetables—peas, onions, beets, chard, turnips, and several kinds of bush beans. And carrots and *lots* of tomatoes, of course. And sometimes oyster plants—"

"Oyster plants?"

Gram smiled up at her. "You probably never heard of it. 'Salsify' is what it's called in seed catalogues, but it's seldom seen anymore. They grow like carrots—long, tapering white roots. Phil liked them cut in crosswise slices, then scalloped or made into a chowder."

"Does it really taste like oysters?"

"Not exactly. But then, unless oysters are eaten raw—which I don't do—their taste's largely from butter and seasonings, whether scalloped or in stew."

Last night, Andi recalled reading in that book about someone eating oyster plant and now, today...

"Our children weren't as fond of it—but we raised enough in those later years so I could freeze some. It made a good lunch for Phil and me...." Her voice faded away and her hands were motionless among the bright pansies. But then she drew in a long breath, shifted position, and returned to weed-pulling.

Andi knew all too well how little things triggered memories, many times about things taken for granted or ones you'd not realized were even retained. "Did you freeze and can other vegetables?"

"Quite a lot—though that gradually decreased.

There's not much point in that once there aren't people to eat it.''

Andi didn't seem to be hitting happy subjects, but she tried once more. "At least Keith enjoys your breakfasts."

"And other meals! And when that boy enjoys something, he lets you know it—which adds to everyone's pleasure."

"Yes. It does." Indeed it does!

Chapter Six

Andi brought up the subject of finances while washing dishes after lunch. "Our arrangement was for breakfast and the use of my room, Gram, but here you are, giving me lunch today and supper on Saturday and snacks..."

"They're on the house."

"They shouldn't be. Especially if I stay a while, which I hope you'll permit."

"Of course I will! I enjoy having you here."

"But this is your business, my dear MaryJean McHenry. And you can't run a business this way."

"And may I remind you that this is *my* business?"

The words were firm, and Andi pursed her lips. "Implying I should mind mine?"

"I wouldn't have put it that way, but since you did—" laughter bubbled to the surface "—it's impolite to argue the fine points of one's wording."

Andi realized that she must insist no further. Once she had her car, she'd take Gram out for a nice meal.

After breakfast, Gram suggested, "Let's go see how Zack and Hal are making out with your car. And then I must go for a trim at The Clip and Curl Joint."

"That's the name of a beauty shop?"

"You'd have to know the owner to appreciate that. When she moved the business from her Third Street home to the shop here on Main, she planned to change it from Betty's Hair Salon to The Clip Joint. It took all us patrons plus her husband to persuade her to add two more words!"

Small towns! thought Andi with amusement. She had assumed the residents would be more stodgy, provincial, perhaps lacking in understanding as well as polish. If Gram's family—her family—was representative, its sense of humor and way of looking at life told an entirely different story!

The car wasn't ready. "One of the boys—Larry," Zack said to Gram, "started to look at it this morning, then had to help with a rush job. I expected to have time for a look-see before this, but things have been hectic."

"That's okay. I've decided to stay for at least a couple more days, and I'd rather it be right than rushed."

"Smart lady!" he approved. "Incidentally, I understand you're having dinner with my son tonight. You tell him his dad says he's to behave himself."

She was momentarily annoyed that others knew of this, then realized Gram's feigned lack of interest made her the obvious talebearer. Gram asked one of the mechanics how his baby was after that bad croup attack, and said she was glad he was better, and would keep praying.

As they came through the showroom, Gram admired the silver luxury model, but shook her head when given the offer of sitting behind the wheel. "You might not get me out—and I'm not about to pay that ridiculous sticker price."

His arm circled her shoulders. "Some day I'll convince you to replace your clunker, Mom. We keep it running, but we'll all feel better when you update."

"Tell you what," she responded, as though offering a new idea, "find me a good, cheap, fairly new one with about forty- or fifty-thousand miles on it. Then maybe we'll discuss it."

Andi smiled, not only at Zack's rising to that bait, but at the thought that MaryJean McHenry might *never* be comfortable paying luxury car prices. No matter how wealthy she became.

Gram pooh-poohed Andi's suggestion about going along to The Clip and Curl Joint, since she was still a stranger and should not be left alone in the house. "You're so smart in some ways, Annie Marker, but that's one of the dumbest things I've heard for a while!"

"Well, I—"

"I know people, and you've got integrity. You're not the type to take what doesn't belong to you."

Andi felt incredibly guilty. Everything this dear lady knew of her was a lie—*except* that she wouldn't steal or use things she discovered for personal gain. "It's possible to trust people too much, dear." That term of affection had slipped out, but she wouldn't retract it if she could.

Gram came to a stop there on the sidewalk, hands

on her hips, purse dangling from the strap around her left wrist. "That's enough of that, Annie. If I didn't want you in my house, believe me, you'd know it."

"I'm sure I would." Yet she felt humbled, unworthy.

Time alone gave her an opportunity to call Dad, and by using her cellular phone she would leave no record.

The answering voice sounded breathless. "I must have taken you away from something, Carol."

"Nothing important. With you away and your father having a dinner meeting, I was polishing the silver."

Carol Winters had been their housekeeper for many years, and lived in her suite on the second floor. Although Andi insisted on arranging for a service to do spring and fall housecleaning, and a caterer to take care of things for major entertaining, Carol, now in her sixties, chose to be in charge of everything else.

"Your father's at work, Andi. I hope this isn't an emergency—I see you're using your special line."

Putting in these unlisted phones upstairs and down must seem strange to Carol, since Andi had said nothing about where she'd be, what she was doing, nor how long she'd be gone. "Does Dad seem...well?"

"I think so. He played golf with the judge on Saturday, went to the office for a few hours yesterday afternoon, and left here about 7:30 this morning."

"Good. And how are you?"

"Fine—as always."

"Get to see your grandnephew yesterday?"

"Oh, yes! I met them for church, then we went out to eat before returning to their place. Little Richie's such a good baby—contented, happy—and laughing out loud already."

"Wonderful." But she couldn't continue small talk; she had no idea how quickly Betty the Beautician would finish Gram's trim. "I'll try reaching Dad at his office, but in case I don't get him, tell him everything's fine with me. And one more thing—he knows my address, and probably the number here at the house, but let me give it to you...."

His private phone was ringing for the fourteenth time when she heard the click of a pickup, then his voice. "Andi?"

"Good afternoon! I almost gave up on your answering."

"I'd asked Ginger to come to the boardroom for me if there was a call here. I'm not as speedy as I once was."

He did sound breathless, but she joked, "In case you hadn't noticed, none of us are." She reminded herself to get on with her message, since he'd be needed in that meeting. "Like we hoped, I did get to stay with MaryJean McHenry. She's delightful and I call her 'Gram,' like not only her family, but half the town apparently does. And of the four generations, I've met all but two members—Bradley and his wife, Paula, the lawyer."

"So how do they strike you thus far—responsible citizens or deadbeats?"

Suspecting from his tone that he was teasing, her answer was almost defensive. "All but Bradley seem to be doing well as to jobs. And I don't know if his being without employment right now is by choice or not."

She briefly told of the picnic, and mentioned going to church with Gram. "And yes, Dad, I still think I'm doing the right thing. In fact, I'm even more convinced of that since Sunday School yesterday."

"Why is that?"

She wanted to tell him about Karlyn's class but said only, "I'll fill you in on that later, when I'm not delaying your meeting. But I wanted you to know all's well at this end."

"I'm glad—for your sake and for theirs. And I do appreciate your calling, princess."

That was what he'd called her when she was little; did he realize he'd said it now? Might that be how he still thought of her? "I know you have my cell phone number, and I gave Carol the one for here at the house—though I'm still asking that you let me call *you*, unless there's trouble."

There was the briefest of pauses, then she heard him say, "I love you, dear. And I do admire what you're doing."

"I admire you, too, Dad, and always have. And I—love you very much."

Why was it easier to say that on the phone than face-to-face? Mother had been the one who never had difficulty telling and showing her love. And why didn't Andi mention that she was going for dinner with Keith?

She'd returned her phone to the drawer, beneath her underclothing, and was sitting in the TV room with a magazine, when Gram came in through the front door. "That's an excellent cut," Andi complimented. "Not everyone can trim wavy hair like yours. And mine."

"I know!" Gram set her bulky purse on the couch. "I tried so many before finding Betty, and I'm sticking with her." She handed Andi a sheet of electric-orange paper. "The flyers for this week are real bright this year, so they stand out when posted on a wall with other advertisements."

"Good idea. And these clever illustrations!" She examined the computer-generated caricatures of a parade, Ferris wheel, hot dog stand, and pony rides. "On the basis of this, *I'd* give your carnival a try."

"Keith will appreciate your thinking that. He didn't want to head up the publicity committee, too, but you know Keith—he can't say No, even when others do."

Andi was not surprised to learn that he took on additional tasks.

If only she'd brought more clothes...but she decided on a white silk top, diaphanous skirt of black-with-tiny-flowers, necklace of multicolored brilliants, and sandals.

She heard Keith before seeing him; a neighbor stopped mowing his yard to call a question about the carnival, and Keith answered before running up the steps, crossing the porch and coming inside. "You look fantastic!"

Could he tell how pleased she was by his reaction? "Is this appropriate for going to your steak house?"

The grin was answer enough, but she appreciated his response. "Or to a Little Theater production, or to a reception for the university president...."

She laughed, at ease again even with his arm around her shoulders, steering her toward the TV room. Having seen and heard everything, Gram agreed, "You do look lovely, Annie—as I already told you."

Andi moved away from Keith to place her hand on the other woman's arm. "Yes, you did. Thank you."

Gram patted her back. "Now you two run along and enjoy yourselves." Laying aside her handwork, Gram followed them to the door. "Just remember that tomorrow's a work day."

They both laughed, and Keith assured her that he'd make it to his office on time. He helped Andi up onto the front seat of the shiny, sand-colored pickup. "She still treats me like a teenager."

"But isn't it nice that she cares that much?"

His eyes were on hers—and he bumped into the door frame. "Now *this* is embarrassing—teenager-ish!—being this clumsy on a first date."

First date. Was this as special to him as to her? she wondered. He closed her door and came around to climb in his own. "I hope you don't mind riding in a truck."

"Not at all. And I've noticed many pickups here."

He wasn't looking at her as he pulled away from the curb. "Probably not this large a percentage in Chicago."

"I doubt it—though I never paid attention."

"Some say it's sort of a macho thing—perhaps an exaggerated proof of masculinity. Or something." The corners of his eyes crinkled as he glanced her way. "And the longer we stay on this topic, the faster you'll agree with Gram that I never *have* grown up."

Her fingertips touched the back of his hand on the

wheel. "She thinks you're terrific, just the way you are."

His hand turned, strong fingers sliding between hers as they came to rest on the seat. There was silence for at least a block, and she wondered if she'd implied that she felt like that, too.

This is weird, she thought. With all the men she'd dated, why—and how—was this happening with Keith? And so quickly? Seeking a safe subject, she told him she liked the carnival flyer Gram had shown her, which led into a discussion of various jobs and responsibilities connected with the annual event.

"Would you be willing to help me with the barbecued chicken Friday night?" he asked. "Or would you rather be with Gram, preparing and serving other parts of the meal?"

Is this your way of asking if I'm staying until then? she wondered. "I think I'd rather help you—but tell me what's involved."

He not only described the process, but went into the story of assisting his father years ago when welding metal bars to make the large grills that were still in service. "Using these each year gives a sense of continuity, being an integral part of the community— the *family* of Sylvan Falls."

She nodded, but said nothing. Not only had he bought that house and put so much of himself into it, but he was completely contented. He'd probably never voluntarily leave.

She felt inexplicably sad. Almost lonely. She shifted on the leather seat, which was a shade darker than the truck's exterior. "Where did you go to college, Keith?"

"Bucknell University."

"Did you stay on campus?"

"The first two years. Then commuted."

Perhaps he'd never really left home, she thought. "And went directly into your present job?"

"Not right away. I got my Master's at Georgia Tech, then worked in New York for a time—before returning home."

"It would be easy to want to remain here."

He squeezed her hand lightly before returning his to the wheel. "Most of my friends don't, however. They leave for college and never come back."

She couldn't interpret the look on his face. Had a special someone been unwilling to stay?

There seemed little need to fill the silence within the smoothly running vehicle. They were nearing a crossroads when he said, "This is it, Annie—The Country Steak House."

The sprawling building on their left was a hodge-podge of add-ons. "They must be very successful."

"They are." He parked some distance from the building, and she released her seat belt, opened her door, and slid down to the macadam. He came around the front of his truck, then tucked her hand through his arm.

A soft breeze played with the short hairs on her forehead, and water from the nearby stream whispered a song as it riffled among rocks. Her voice was as soft as the water's as she breathed, "What a perfect evening."

"Yes." He led her toward the edge of the parking lot, and she stood there looking down at the creek before glancing over at him. How long had he been looking at *her* instead of all this beauty? "I like your world, Keith. Very much."

"I'm glad."

His arm drew her hand closer, and she felt the regular beating of his heart—or was it her own?

"Bored?"

Had her slow exhalation registered as a sigh? "Not at all. I just feel...perfectly content."

"Me, too, Annie," he said, then repeated it, perhaps surprised by his own statement. "Me, too."

Several couples greeted them as they went inside, and she found herself introduced again as Gram's friend. But when the owner came to their corner table shortly after they were seated, Keith said, "Annie, I'd like you to meet Rob Templeton, my scout leader for years and good friend ever since. Rob, my new friend, Annie Marker."

Their "I'm pleased to meet you" was a duet, and they smiled in acknowledgment. He accepted their invitation to join them, and Andi became aware of Rob's skill at drawing people out. In the short time he was with them, he learned where she was from, her version of how she happened to be here, her educational background...

For her part, she discovered that his daughter was his partner and head chef, and that his second son, now a doctor in Virginia, had been Keith's closest friend.

He excused himself after wishing Andi a good stay, and within a minute or two, a very attractive brown-eyed woman, a feminine version of her tall, dark-complexioned father, came hurrying from the kitchen. Keith got to his feet and met her with a hug, while she was yet a few steps from their table. Gretchen's last name was Bigalow, and she had two children—but no mention was made of a husband.

From the beginning, Andi had been aware of the sound of sizzling, and now watched as their sirloins were grilled to perfection—medium well for her, medium rare for him. During this wait, they made their own salads from crispy fresh vegetables, and chose from assorted side dishes.

The steaks were presented on hot, heavy platters that resembled pewter. "I can't believe I ordered one this big!"

"They're sorta like Christmas trees—they grow after they're chosen," he said dryly—and that led into a sharing of Christmas customs and activities.

Actually, she kept *him* on that subject, and again became aware of how much she'd missed by not knowing these relatives.

"You're just picking at your food. Don't you like it?"

She hadn't realized how enthralled she'd been. "I was so interested in your stories that I forgot to eat."

He pretended a frown. "If my talking's keeping you from enjoying your steak, I'd better shut up."

With exaggerated meekness, she assured him she'd do better in the future, and dutifully cut off another bite-size portion, which she ate as he began yet another account of a holiday get-together.

Their young waitress refilled their glasses with iced tea several times, assuring them that it was quite all right to stay as long as they'd like. But when Andi finally glanced at her watch, her shocked gaze rose to meet his. "I can't believe it's past eleven!"

The slow smile, the crinkles at the outer corners of his expressive brown eyes... "You have a way of making time fly, Annie Marker."

There was a stab of almost-pain in her chest, gratitude that he'd apparently enjoyed their time together, but sadness that she was still playing a part. "As Gram reminded us," she said, pushing back her chair, "tomorrow's a working day for you."

"If anyone else said that, I'd be annoyed, but never with Gram." He got to his feet, too. "Or you."

Her eyes met his across the table, and she had difficulty getting out even something simple. "At least I'm in good company—with Gram."

They didn't talk much on the drive home, but there was a comfortable, relaxed feeling. This remained even as they got out of the pickup, walked up the steps, and stood facing one another, both of her hands in his. "I've enjoyed this evening with you, Keith— the dinner, conversation...everything. Thank you."

"Likewise, Annie." His head inclined slightly and his fingers tightened around hers. "Thanks for coming with me."

She forced herself to resist what *might* have been a little pull—his drawing her toward himself. Even if he were, she told herself, she must not let herself get into something that could drastically alter her situation. "Good night, Keith. Sleep well."

Another quick pressure of his hands on hers, and he released them. "I'm sure I will. You do the same...."

Lying in bed later, she considered things she might have shared with him, had she wished to. Among these were times she'd gone on trips or done fun

things with friends during Christmas vacations. And
Dad's being in Hong Kong and London and Rome
for various holidays.

As to entertaining done at home during the later
years, Mother hired a decorator who one time brought
in a twelve-foot modernistic white tree. And there was
that tricolor one the year the French ambassador was
their guest.

Andi tossed and turned before finally drifting off.
In her dream she was perhaps six, and going with
Mother to some Christmas tree farm where she
walked, ran, and climbed hills, looking for a perfect
little tree to cut and bring home. And she watched
Mother count out coins to pay for it.

The tree almost reached the ceiling when placed
upon a stand, and Mother and Andi decorated it with
several strings of lights and some glass balls and paper snowflakes. Andi begged to stay up till Daddy got
home to see it, but fell asleep on the couch.

When he came, Daddy picked her up and held her
close—so tight it was almost difficult to breathe. He
said the tree was beautiful and *she* was beautiful, but
then—and she didn't know why—he began to cry.
And Mother came to them and she was crying, too,
and so was Andi.

Yet it had seemed to be a most wonderful Christmas.

Chapter Seven

Morning—another sunny one.

Andi padded down the stairs, barefoot, light robe over her pajamas, and saw Gram again on her knees in the back yard, weeding the flower bed around a large magnolia tree. Andi microwaved a mug of water, dropped in a tea bag, headed back upstairs, and closed her door.

It was 6:46 in Chicago; Dad should still be at home. But it was again Carol whom Andi greeted with, "Good morning. I hope I didn't wake you."

"It *is* a good morning, Andi, since it's you," the cheerful voice agreed. "You know I'm always around by now."

"Has Dad left already?"

"I don't think so, but I'll check...."

He was soon on the line. "Andi! I hope nothing's wrong."

"Everything's great. But Gram's outside, working

with her flowers, so this seemed a good time to talk. We didn't have much opportunity yesterday.''

Was there a slight pause? Was he also under time pressure now? His words didn't seem to indicate that. ''You're enjoying yourself?''

''More than I expected, or even hoped for! We have some really fine relatives, Dad. I wish you knew them.''

This time there was a definite hesitation, as though he was deciding what to say. ''I doubt that would be wise under present circumstances.''

''Probably not. Not right now.'' Will it ever be possible to meet as relatives? she wondered. She was unprepared for the wrench she felt at the idea that it might not happen. ''I had a strange dream last night. It seems like a remembrance, but I'm not sure.''

''Want to tell me about it?''

His voice and manner made her think that he was smiling. She hoped so, anyway. ''Keith was talking last night about family Christmases, so that's probably what triggered this. I was with Mother, looking for a tree in someone's field. We brought it home and set it on a table and decorated it.

''You came back from work and I was so excited about showing you what we'd done, and you said it was pretty, and that you liked it, and you picked me up and held me.

''But then you started to cry and so did I—and then Mother was hugging us, and we were *all* crying....'' She felt moisture in her eyes now, after all these years. Would Dad think her foolish?

She heard him clearing his throat. ''It *is* a memory—one I haven't thought about for a long time.''

It was hard to wait for him to continue. "That was one of our darkest Christmases, Andrea."

He's calling me by my given name, she realized, the name given because Mother had such a hard time giving birth—there would be no sons to carry on his name, no more children at all.

"We'd sunk everything in the effort to start the electronics business, and it looked like it just might work, but we couldn't be sure. You wanted a tree so badly—said all your friends were having them, and then a neighbor said someone she knew was going out of tree farming and was selling what were left for practically nothing. She invited you two to go with her."

Are you waiting for me to respond? she asked silently. I don't know what to say....

"Seeing your happiness with the tree and our being together made me aware of what we'd been missing by my workaholism—but I'd been trying so *hard* to make life better for all of us...."

Her tears had not fallen; there was even a little smile on her lips. "I don't recall feeling resentful or sad."

"We went, together, to a Christmas Eve service at the church on the corner, and the next day—the only one in years when I didn't go to the plant for at least a while—we took a long walk together, and we talked and sang Christmas carols and other songs...."

"I *remember* that now—I *do*." Some of the excitement came back to her even now. "It was wonderful having you with us all that day."

"It was the only thing I had to give—myself."

"It was all we needed," she replied.

* * *

Her tea was tepid, no longer appealing. However, she decided to get ready for the day before going downstairs—and Gram was inside by then.

Andi said she'd be more than satisfied with packaged cereal and fruit, but Gram insisted on fixing oatmeal with raisins for herself, anyway. Together, they ate it at the kitchen table.

Gram placed her spoon back in her empty bowl. "I wonder if they're working on your car this morning."

"Eager to get rid of me?"

Gram clucked her tongue reprovingly. "You're looking for compliments—but I admit to hoping you'll recuperate here instead of gallivanting off to New England, all alone."

Andi smiled. "I've agreed to help Keith grill chickens on Friday—whatever's involved with that. So I guess you're stuck with me till then, anyway."

"Good!" Gram pushed back her chair. "In the meantime, do whatever you'd like—rest, read, go for a walk."

"What are your plans for today?"

"Well, we have to eat lunch either early or late. My literacy session's scheduled from twelve till one."

"Literacy session?"

"I've volunteered for years, teaching adults. There are few things that give me more satisfaction than seeing letters and words and meanings come to life for people who couldn't read before."

"It's hard to imagine—being unable to read."

"Isn't that the truth! Well, because of this program there are thousands—maybe tens or hundreds of thousands—who not only get more challenging and higher-paying jobs, but can shop better and help their kids with homework.''

While Gram got her shower and did tasks around the kitchen, Andi washed their few dishes and swept the kitchen floor. Then she took a long, meandering walk through this end of town. Later, after eating a sandwich, she walked Gram to the library and went on to the post office on South Main.

On the way back, she entered a building where fabrics and craft supplies were displayed behind one plate glass window, while housewares, clothing, and children's clothing filled the other.

This place must be old, she decided, for the faded, fancily painted sign above the windows read, Nathan's 5 and 10 Cent Store. She smiled in response to a cheerful ''Good morning,'' before the sixtyish woman glanced at her watch and, coming from behind the checkout counter, corrected herself. ''I see it's already afternoon.''

''And a lovely one it is,'' Andi agreed, hoping to encourage conversation. The name on the identification badge said Lois, and it wasn't long before Andi was addressing her that way, telling the woman of her car problem and of staying at Gram's bed-and-breakfast.

''That's too bad—about the car, I mean.'' Lois was then all smiles in speaking of Gram. ''She's one fine woman, always doin' for others, even when she doesn't have to.''

Andi started slowly back down the first aisle, picking up an occasional item, looking at, then replacing it. "She's at the library right now, helping someone learn to read."

"She did that even before Phil was killed."

Andi's hand hovered over a boxed set of miniature characters before lifting it. "She mentioned his dying suddenly...." she began, hoping for more information.

"It was terrible! *Awful.*" A shudder ran through her. "Phil was our fire chief—we have a volunteer company here, y'know—and he was excellent, one of the very best.

"He really worked with the guys—and it was while he was chief they started takin' in women, and boys over 16, makin' them practice all the time, and gettin' them to take special courses. It was 'cause of his pushin' so hard that they started winning awards year after year."

Her voice lowered. "The day he died, he was inside the burning mill, tryin' to get a man out, when it collapsed."

Feeling chilled to the bone, Andi wrapped her arms around herself. "How awful!"

"Gram was there. She and a couple others was makin' coffee and sandwiches for the firefighters—"

"Oh, no!" That poor, dear woman! she thought, her heart going out to Gram.

"She saw Phil go in—but it wasn't till the next day they got him back out. His burned body was over the other man—even at the end tryin' to protect someone else."

Tears filled Andi's eyes, and her throat felt tight. "She didn't tell me...."

"She wouldn't. And she prob'ly didn't mention

that the new fire hall has his name—it's sort of a memorial to him.''

A customer was coming in the front door, and Lois went to greet him. Andi stood there, eyes focused unseeingly on the silly little plastic figures she'd almost forgotten she was holding. Gram had said that first morning that she always prayed for the firemen; how she must have prayed for her beloved husband!

Why did he have to die like that, God? Why didn't you save him when he was trying to do what he thought was right? And Mother—why did she have to die so young? And Jon, even younger? And....

With robotic preciseness, Andi fit the box into its niche among the others, and returned to the front of the store by way of a parallel aisle. She did not feel up to more than raising her hand in farewell and trying to smile.

She walked to the large brick-and-glass library. From the fiction section, where she wasn't actually checking anything, she could see Gram sitting with a tall, muscular, black-haired man whom she guessed to be in his late thirties. She couldn't make out many words, but was aware of his extra-careful enunciation.

Gram was beaming as he relaxed back against his chair. ''Well done, Joe. I can tell you've been practicing!''

''It's worth it, Gram. You have no idea how great it felt the other night to read a new book to my little Betsy—a book I'd never even *looked* at before.''

''You're going to have many of those good experiences.''

''But—'' he looked concerned ''—I can keep on

coming, can't I? Even though I'm reading some better?''

"Of course you can. We still have many things to work on, and I plan to continue till you're reading with as much skill and speed and understanding as I have."

After tutor and student walked together to the front door, Gram returned to talk with the librarian. From there, she asked Andi if she'd found books she'd like to check out.

"Not today." Replacing the one she'd been looking at, she crossed to the women. "For one thing, I don't have a library card."

"You can use mine," Gram offered, glancing from her to the woman behind the desk.

"I haven't started those I brought with me, and there's a whole bookcase full of interesting volumes just outside my bedroom door."

On the way home—yes, it almost feels like home, Andi thought—Gram explained that Joe had been studying with her for over a year, after nearly losing his job as a long-distance truck driver because of difficulty reading instructions and keeping travel logs. He'd been incredibly lucky until making a costly mistake. "He never learned to sound out words, and some addresses are hard. He was too scared to ask for help—afraid to let anyone know he couldn't read."

Andi nodded. "I heard him mention a child— Betsy. Are there more?"

"Two others, in middle and high school. At first they were ashamed about their dad, but no more! His family's been to my place for dinner, and now understand and are proud of what he's accomplishing!"

"Gram, I'm truly honored to know you." She *nearly* said she felt honored to be part of her family!

"And I'm truly sorry for you if you have to be 'honored' by knowing someone like me," Gram responded crisply. "I'm just an ordinary woman in an ordinary town...." But then she corrected herself. "I got that last wrong—our *town* is *extra*ordinary."

Andi nodded agreement to the latter—and didn't argue the former. She *knew* Gram to be special.

Zack, wearing tan coveralls under which she saw the collar of a blue-striped shirt, greeted them as they walked through the garage's big open doors. He kissed his mother and grinned at Andi. "It's fixed!"

"What caused the problem?" She was almost afraid to ask, but he'd expect the question.

He frowned slightly. "I must admit it was something we could have done—just a belt that loosened enough to slip."

Her smile was partly because of this proof of his honesty. He could have made up any story and charged whatever he chose. "I'm grateful for your fixing it—and for its giving me time to get acquainted with your town."

"You don't have to rush off now that it's taken care of, do you?"

"Not right away."

Gram added, "She's helping Keith barbecue chicken Friday."

"*He's* not so dumb." Zack chuckled. "Must take after his old man."

Andi smiled. "I've never been to a carnival like this."

"I think you'll like it. In a way, it's a slice of the America of several generations ago—when people in a community still worked together for a worthwhile project and managed to have fun doing it."

"I'm looking forward to it." It was her turn to push a little. "How are you coming with your parade floats?"

"Two down, one to go."

"Which still needs finishing?"

"I'll bet it's *this* one, isn't it?" Gram was feigning annoyance. "The one for your garage?"

He assumed a hurt, little-boy look, lower lip thrust out. "But it's almost done, Mom. Honest."

One of the mechanics stage-whispered from where he was working nearby on the red sedan. "We hope that means we won't have to stay *too* late tonight to finish it."

Keith did not come that evening, nor phone. Gram received other calls, each ring giving Andi hope—which was immediately dashed. The first concerned someone's bringing onions for the hamburger barbecue Gram was to prepare. The second had something to do with her Sunday School class. And the third was from Brad, the relative she hadn't met.

"Oh, I'm sorry, dear," Gram was saying. "Do you have other good leads?"

Trouble with his job search, Andi surmised, hoping her eavesdropping wasn't too obvious.

"I don't know him or, rather, *he* wouldn't know *me*—but I think he's some relation of Betty, who cuts my hair. Maybe she could…All right, dear, I understand your wanting to handle it yourself.''

It was several minutes before she hung up. ''Poor Brad! The jobs he thinks he'd like require skills he doesn't have, and his skills don't lead to anything challenging enough for him, nor earn a big enough salary.''

''Does he…*need* a big salary?''

''Not to support his family. But to *not* earn big bucks is hard on his self-esteem.''

''Oh.''

''He and Paula met in college, fell head-over-heels in love, and got married. They were both excellent students, but he was a year behind, because of the way their birthdays fell. When she got accepted at law school, he dropped out, got a job to support them—and, having been in ROTC, got called into military service during an emergency.

''He never quite caught up with life after that.''

Andi waited, unsure about asking questions. The older woman finally added, ''Vanessa was born during Paula's last year in law school. Paula was so busy that it was Brad who raised her. So she and her dad are still especially close.''

Andi would have liked to bridge the silence, but couldn't imagine what might fill it properly.

''Maybe it would have been better if Vanessa weren't so beautiful. There's something wrong there again.…''

Again?

''She barely spoke to anyone but Keith on Sunday.'' She exhaled forcefully. ''She's always followed him around like a puppy, ever since she could toddle. That's probably how she got so interested in computers, seeing how involved he's always been. She'd be playing games on his, drawing, and doing all sorts of stuff instead of being outside playing.''

"She was something of a loner?'' Andi asked.

"I think so. Paula doesn't. She's sure her daughter's 'happy and fulfilled'—why wouldn't she be, with fellows calling and wanting to date her ever since middle school? But Vanessa's unhappy—has been for years. Sometimes I sense turmoil—desperation, almost.''

Perhaps having a big, close family is only a mixed blessing, thought Andi. It hurts terribly to love this much.

During the next morning's call, she asked Dad how things were going at the plant—and this time quizzed him on exactly how he was feeling and whether he was getting enough exercise. And relaxation.

"Since I have no real I.D. by which people could get in touch in case they need to,'' she said near the end of their conversation, "I've given Gram this new number. Is it okay to also give your private one at work?''

He hesitated only a moment. "Do that—but tell MaryJean to use it only for a real emergency. Otherwise, Carol will get in touch, and I'll return the call.''

"And you still want any mail for you—as Andrew Marker—to be sent to the judge's address?''

"He'll get it to me immediately.''

Her little cough was an attempt to cover almost-embarrassment. "I know it's essential to stick to the original plans—but I'm feeling more and more guilty.''

''Wanta call it off?''

''I can't. By now I've learned that none of them probably *need* our money. And at least Gram and Keith would undoubtedly give much of it away if they had it.''

''That bothers you?''

''Not the way they'd do it—actually, it's more personal their way, rather than by a foundation.''

''So?''

She exhaled forcefully, not realizing she'd done that until she heard the sound reverberate through the earpiece. ''I'm helping Keith grill chickens for the carnival tomorrow night.''

He chuckled. ''Taking advantage of all *kinds* of learning opportunities, aren't you?''

''You could call it that.'' But she could call it lots of other things, too. Like enjoying the opportunity of being with Keith. Like doing something with him that he enjoyed. Like getting to know the people of the community better—through Keith, who was so well liked.

Chapter Eight

It was sunny and bright in central Pennsylvania, so Andi thought little of Dad's mentioning rain in Chicago. By the following morning, weather predictions for evening were anything but favorable.

Nevertheless, as Gram browned package after package of hamburger in big iron skillets, Andi worked with onions until tears were running down her cheeks. She'd never so much as chopped a raw onion, or removed one's outer layers—and found this traumatic.

When Gram asked if she'd like to trade jobs, however, Andi blotted her face with the soft, hand-embroidered tea towel, which soaked up moisture better than the tissues she'd tried. "No, thanks. I only have a few more, then I'll thoroughly wash my hands and eyes and face before starting the celery."

Rain began to sheet downward, but she refrained from asking the obvious question. She was nearly finished chopping the second stalk when the phone rang and Andi answered for Gram. "...I don't know yet, but I'll ask."

"It's Leona Topfer," she relayed, "wanting to know if everything's 'off' for tonight."

"I'll speak to her," Gram replied as she continued turning ground beef with a spatula. Andi handed over the portable phone. "Hi, Leona. Sorta wet out there, isn't it...? But I was talking to Hank Jenkins yesterday, and he was complaining about how his corn and oats, especially, need rain... Oh, I wouldn't say that—and of *course* we'll still have the dinner. Maybe not as many will come if the parade's canceled, but let's not cross that bridge yet...."

Gram groaned when many others showed their concern by phoning. "I'm about ready to take that thing off the hook! You'd think *I'm* the one making decisions, and I'm just the barbecue-maker and helper with the dinner!"

Andi laughed. "*Just* has got to be the wrong word. You're more involved than you let on."

She didn't respond right away, and sounded subdued when admitting, "I guess I am. I wanted to be a good helpmate to Phil, so did everything I could while he was fire chief."

Andi kept on working at the galvanized sink, hoping Gram would continue—yet almost relieved that this was not to be the time for talking about her husband's death.

"Bud Simpson became chief after that. His wife had her hands full with their three little girls, so he asked me to continue heading up the Auxiliary. Though I haven't been president for years, I do seem to have a lot of input—more than I should."

"I'm sure they're grateful for all you do."

"But it's probably not good for the organization. I'm in my seventies, you know. I do want to contribute, but I've been thinking it's time to step back and let younger folk have their turn."

"They'll resist."

"So be it." She shrugged. "I'm ready to pass on Phil's recipes to someone else—"

"You still make this barbecue from his recipe?"

She nodded. "And you'll be using his for the barbecue sauce for the chicken tonight. He tried dozens, maybe hundreds, of recipes before he was satisfied. Everyone raved about them, so he always took care of making them.

"But *I* do just the hamburg barbecue. Usually."

Andi saw her look toward the many glass jars of what looked like tomato puree. "You provide the ingredients?"

"The meat's reimbursed from the profits and the onions are donated. As for tomatoes—one of the growers for Mario's Italian Products, in Petersgrove, contributes those. Stan calls when he's finished harvesting—when it's not profitable to pick again. A bunch of us get together and go there and bring back *bushels,* and several women come here and we make puree for the barbecue and can the thinner portion to use as an appetizer at meals we serve."

"That's very generous."

"Stan even tells people to take what they can use for themselves, or to share with others."

Andi didn't embarrass her by saying her reference had been to the work of the women, as much as to the grower's gift. "So, much of Sylvan Falls's pasta throughout the year is topped with products made from Stan's tomatoes.''

''Right you are!'' Gram pushed the skillet onto a cool burner before transferring the browned meat into one of the kettles containing what had already been browned. Andi's chopped onions were then dumped into the frying pan. ''I'll brown these, too, before putting them with the meat, but will only finish off one big batch of barbecue till we have a better idea of what's happening this evening.''

The phone rang and Andi picked up again. ''Hi, Keith! Everyone's been wondering about tonight.''

He chuckled. ''And a good morning to you, as well.''

''Sorry!'' she responded, feeling nothing but happiness. ''I do wish you a good morning, and—'' seeing the woman's smile ''—Gram does, too.''

''That's better. So now I'll fill you in as well as I can. A number of us have been on the phone and made the decision that the parade has to be postponed—''

''Oh, that's too bad!''

''That's for sure. You have no idea how much work goes into creating those floats. Rain does awful things to crepe-paper roses and tissue-covered wagons or flatbeds.''

''Oh.'' She'd been thinking only of people getting wet.

''Tell Gram that dinner's still scheduled—and we'll need some of her barbecue.'' He drew in an audible breath. ''Have you had the radio or TV on?''

''No, we've been busy—and talking.''

''Well, we're trying to saturate the area with notices. We can't expect as good a turnout as if we had the parade and the rides, but I'm planning to leave here early. How 'bout I pick you up around 3:30?''

Andi knew she'd love that but said, ''You'll have lots of other things to take care of, so I'll walk over and meet you at the lot.''

''Well…''

She couldn't tell if that betrayed relief—or regret. ''Should I be there by 3:30?''

''That would be great. Several retired men will have the fires started, so we can get right to work.''

His final words, ''I do appreciate you, Annie Marker!'' made her smile as she hung up the phone. She'd have liked to tell him that she appreciated *him*, as well, but that was not appropriate.

''I should have asked what to wear,'' she fretted later.

''Anything serviceable.'' Gram had no hesitation about giving advice. ''Something that won't be hurt by getting dirty. And greasy.''

''Jeans okay?''

''Most appropriate. And a lightweight top. You'll be hot and sweaty before you're done.''

Andi remembered that comment a number of times throughout late afternoon and evening. The rain did stop around six, but the unmoving air was heavy with moisture.

Someone had already washed the first case of chicken breast and leg quarters, so as soon as she arrived, she helped place these on one of the huge, heavy, welded grids, put another on top, and secured the metal clips around all four sides to keep the meat in place.

As these began sizzling over the charcoal pit, she assisted with setting up the second one, then offered to go inside the fire hall—the Philip James McHenry Memorial Hall—to wash chicken from another 40-pound carton.

Although expecting the job to be boring, she found it almost fun as she worked near some of the older women and men. They were busily talking and visiting while preparing bowls of mashed potatoes, corn, peas, baked beans, bread and rolls, and a colorful salad called "church cabbage."

Junior firemen, and other men and women, carried these to the long tables where happy, hungry people were being served family-style—then brought back empty dishes for refills.

Gram wiped her face with the hem of her apron as she paused by the deep sink where Andi was scrubbing her fourth case of chicken pieces. "Those media blurbs must have been really something! We usually serve four hundred to six hundred dinners on *beautiful* nights, and we must be nearly to four hundred already."

Andi saw Keith coming through the dining area, looking handsome and happy as he stopped to chat briefly with some, and to respond to calls from others on his way to where she was working. "Ah, you have a couple more bucketfuls ready!"

She'd have preferred to be outside, working with him under the tent, but asked, "Do you need more right away?"

"We haven't decided yet. The crowd's been great, but by the time these—" he hefted the five-gallon pails ''—get cooked and served, we may have all we need.''

''However,'' an older man said, ''we sell the extra barbecued chicken at much more than we'd get for raw.''

Gram started to say something, but, looking somewhat sheepishly at Andi, backed away and kept herself out of the discussion. The majority of those in the kitchen argued for continuing the cooking, Gram's only contribution being an enquiry as to whether there was enough sauce.

Andi almost requested a trade-off with someone working at the grills—but was grateful she hadn't when Keith returned, saying he was helping her finish the job. ''This hasn't been much fun for you.''

She was so pleased that it was no stretch to assert that she was enjoying her first carnival experience.

His beautifully sculpted lips curved upward, and his brown eyes shone in the artificial light. ''Are you always such a good sport?''

''Because I'm scrubbing chickens?''

''Because of doing that when you had every reason to expect to be out at the grill, meeting people.''

''I'd never done either before.''

''All the more reason we should have kept you there.'' His tone was decisive, but he went on before she responded. ''At least we're almost done here, so we'll both go finish making the best barbecued chicken ever! And then, after we eat some of it— which is one of the perks—and if it clears off—which it looks like it may—we'll take some rides, too.''

She kept her voice light. ''What nice perks these are!''

Time flew with him beside her, literally rubbing shoulders. When they finished, she quickly scoured the sink, then washed and dried her hands.

She joined him at the grills, and he teased her about her "masterful job" of carefully placing each quarter-chicken. But she didn't stay long this time, for Keith went with her into the dining area. She felt almost as excited as when Mother took her to the fair back when she was nine—too filled with wonder and the enjoyment of people watching to be hungry.

"Come on, Annie, eat up!" Keith coaxed, holding a spoonful of baked beans an inch or two above her plate. "You deserve it after all your work."

She accepted it, and added a small amount of peas and of church cabbage, all of which was delicious. Keith, carrying on a conversation with people across the table, was distracted enough not to notice at first how little she was eating. When he did, she begged off. "I saw those pies in the kitchen and am saving room for mincemeat—or maybe I'll try what someone called 'shoofly.'"

"My favorite's apple," Keith announced, and others asked if she'd seen coconut custard and lemon chiffon.

When she said there had been some of these and others when she was there, Keith called to a teen carrying a tray filled with dessert plates, to ask about all five varieties.

Rocky lowered his tray. "Here's apple, shoofly and lemon. Take what you want, and I'll check on the others."

She should have canceled the mince, but ended up eating that as well as the delicious crumb-and-molasses concoction. Leaning back in her chair, she sighed with contentment. "I've never before eaten two pieces of pie at one sitting!"

Keith grinned. "Then it's about time, Annie. You're probably the only adult here who could make that statement."

As they left the building, Annie commented again on all the red fire equipment parked close to the street, making room inside for barbecue, ice cream and hot dog stands. A ball-toss game was set up on the macadam, and useful and novelty items were on sale at the booth where chances were being sold, the prize being the displayed hand-stitched, appliqued quilt.

"This is outstanding." Andi examined the individual blocks, representing all remaining covered bridges in the area. "The needlework's so fine and even."

"Ever since the 1976 Bicentennial, The Sylvan Quilters meet all year round. In addition to projects of their own, they always make a couple major works, like this."

"And donate them for this cause?"

"They always give one for us to chance-off. And they have other pet projects, like last fall when they did a most beautiful original, with angels. Everyone who saw it wanted it, so they raised a good part of what was needed for a local girl's bone marrow transplant."

"What a marvelous gift—and what moral support, in addition to the financial one." She was liking this town more and more. "Is she well now?"

"She's better, though there's still a ways to go."

She'd been aware of the distinctive, brightly joyful calliope music as background for the happy sounds of the crowd, which had been increasing since the rain stopped. As they approached the merry-go-round, she observed riders on horses, as well as dolphins, unicorns, tigers and other creatures.

"That little fellow isn't enjoying this much." She nodded toward a crying child perhaps a year old, being held on the back of a jovial-appearing lion—and comforted by his young mother.

Keith squeezed Andi's hand, which he'd been holding since they'd checked back at the grill, where late-arriving volunteers were finishing the cleanup. "Ah, but his grandparents are," he said, pointing to a couple snapping pictures. "As he gets older, he'll enjoy looking at those and hearing about his very first Sylvan Falls carnival."

Are Chicagoans this proud of our city? Andi wondered. Some must be, although those in her own social and business circles didn't talk about it much. However there were all those arts, philanthropic institutions, sports...

"...do you prefer?"

She'd been wool-gathering! "What did you say?"

"I'm really losing it." He stood there looking down at her, feigning dismay. "I can't even keep your attention while holding your hand and offering you the fabulous creature of your choice to ride upon."

She started to laugh. "You needn't worry about that, Keith—'losing it'!" As unselfconsciously as though she were with Dad—or Jon—she found herself pulled close, cheek against his.

For just a moment she remained there, until, realizing what she'd done, she drew back, a little embarrassed and too aware of her rapid heartbeat. But the smile was still on her face as he asked, "Because I never really *had* it?"

"Hardly!" Sobering, she explained, "I was thinking of your town, your people, and your being such a part of it. You relate to all this, to them, in such real ways. Caring. Working. I don't know..." Words failed her—and that bothered her. Andi was used to handling conversation well.

"I—don't know what to say," he stammered.

So he, too, had this difficulty. This time her fingers tightened around his. "Nothing's required. You are who and what you are—which is very good."

Was there ever such a creature as fabulous as the unicorn on which she rode? Or the dragon beside her, serving as Keith's steed? Was ever a ride more joyful?

They did not talk much—didn't need to. She waved to Jake and Traci, who were obviously coaxing their mother to buy tickets. The line of those impatiently waiting grew longer, and the carousel slowed and stopped.

Keith's strong hands around her waist assisted her to dismount, and his left one remained, warm against her waist. They spoke to Karlyn for a minute or so, and to Gram, who'd finished her food-preparation duties and was about to leave.

Keith seemed to know everyone, and engaged in conversation as they waited in line to ride in one of the enclosed, rocket-shaped pods at the end of long projections. She wondered why she even considered this monstrosity—then became almost grateful for the centrifugal force throwing her against him, again and again, and keeping her there, breathless, before occasional reprieves.

"Wow! I didn't realize it would be like *that*," Andi exclaimed as they climbed out after the ride—too long as far as comfort was concerned, too short for the physical closeness forced upon them.

She told him that she'd prefer not to go on other rides tonight. "But you may if you like, perhaps with your nieces and nephews."

"Sure I will," he scoffed. "You worked your fingers to the bone and now I'm supposed to take the *kids* for rides?"

"Well, if I weren't here, I'll bet you'd be with them." Though maybe you'd be with some other woman, she thought.

"But they're here all the time, ready and eager to do things with me. And I have the uneasy feeling that you're about to slip away at any moment."

She permitted his talking her into one more ride— the Ferris wheel—and tried to ignore the wind, which had begun blowing more briskly. With all the music and the flashing lights from the rides, and all the people laughing and talking, time passed quickly.

The huge upright wheel stopped, people got out of the seat at the bottom, and she and Keith sat down. The attendant secured the safety rod across them, and then they started to rise, to go around.

Keith made their seat rock by leaning forward and back and pushing with his feet. "I always did this as a kid."

"Behave yourself!" She elbowed him. "The idea of this ride is for the compartment to remain horizon-

tal as the wheel goes around. And the riders are supposed to *enjoy* themselves.''

He relaxed against the seat, arm around the back
of where she was sitting. ''When our car reaches the
top, we'll have quite a view. Let's get comfortable
and enjoy the ride.''

That's when she noticed the flash of lightning
which, from their position at the top of the wheel,
seemed to light up everything. Startled, she asked, ''Is
that as near at it appears?''

He was looking beyond her, toward the next forked
bolt crossing the sky. He nodded and, as they approached the bottom, called to the ride's operator.
''Better get everyone off, Larry. A severe electrical
storm's coming from the west, almost here.''

The young man glanced around before hurrying to
the ball-throwing area. Andi and Keith were at the
top again, wind whipping their hair and clothing, by
the time he and an older man came running back.
Stopping the wheel at each seat, they asked people to
leave, and Andi was grateful to step down onto the
small platform, then to the ground.

The first drops were falling, and people looked up,
surprised, then gathered families, if they had them,
and dashed for cars, most getting soaked by the down-
pour before getting away from the grounds. Keith and
Andi ran first to the open-sided barbecued-chicken
tent—but its protection was minimal—wind-driven
rain pelted them.

At the first slight lull, they hurried to the building
where the food had been served—and found many
others there, also shivering from wet garments and
hair.

There was an eeriness about the place now that the calliope and other music was shut off. There was no more calling out of those hawking hot dogs, barbecues and ice cream, or barkers enticing the crowd to take a chance and win a prize.

Andi was aware of the almost continuous roll of thunder. A phone rang and the tension was palpable—until the fireman who answered reported it to be the wife of one of the men, asking him to pick up milk on his way home! She knew the laughter and teasing were at least partly from relief that nobody had to go out in this storm because of a fire or accident.

The second call, however, was a request for an ambulance to come to the home of an elderly man known to have a bad heart. Two men and a woman left immediately, the powerful equipment pulling onto the street, then turning left toward the highway by which Andi had entered this town—not even a week earlier!

She and Keith waited for the storm to let up a little, then hurried, as quickly as Andi could manage, toward Gram's. Then the rain was again pouring down.

Her leg had been feeling better than she'd have thought possible, but she was soon forced to slow to a walk. She pushed her dripping hair back away from her face. "I don't think we *can* get wetter, anyway."

"I was thinking the same, so—" he swung their clasped hands back and forth "—let's just enjoy our stroll."

"I'd enjoy it more if the lightning would let up. I love these old trees along your streets—but do have a healthy respect for what could happen if one gets struck!"

"You're right. Let's go down this alley and enter Gram's from the rear."

Although most of the backyards were free of tall trees, power lines were strung along one side. In an effort to stop thinking of them, she said, "I was wondering—I see you have women in your fire company. You haven't had trouble with terms like *Firemen's* Carnival and *Firemen's* Parade?"

"Not much—and don't bring it up! This is so traditional that nobody's seriously considered *Firepeople's* or anything. And the fire company's just that— The Sylvan Falls Fire Company. That's about as inclusive as one can get."

They hurried up the walk, and he reached to open the door. Sliding out of her shoes, she stepped on the throw rug inside. "Gra-am! We're back—and dripping all over your nice clean floor."

"Stay there, Annie." The call was followed by hurried footsteps, then Gram in the kitchen doorway. "I'll bring towels for you, and for my all-wet grandson."

"No argument as to my being all wet, but I'm not staying this time."

Andi looked around quickly, not expecting that. "I—suppose you have another big day tomorrow."

"And I must get up especially early."

"You don't have to go to work, do you?" Gram asked.

"Not this weekend. But I have some personal business to take care of." He smiled, said, "Sleep well," and closed the door.

Andi realized that Gram's gaze remained on the closed door as Keith's footsteps became less audible.

Was she, too, wondering about Keith's personal business?

Was it something to do with his "unbreakable date"? And why must it be taken care of "especially early"?

"Would it be indecent to take off my jeans here, since they're so wet and dirty? I could wrap the towel around myself and run upstairs...."

"Good idea," the older woman agreed. "We'll leave them on the sink, and tomorrow morning you can run a load of laundry—or several, if you want to."

"I'd appreciate that." Andi draped her leather belt over the back of a kitchen chair, unzipped her jeans and tugged them off. "I thought I was bringing enough clothing, but will soon be out of jeans and shirts."

A few minutes later, she was soaking in a tub of hot water, not only getting clean, but warm—which seemed equally important. She was certainly tired enough, but knew she wouldn't be able to sleep right away.

She read only two more short chapters, however, before laying *Aikenside* on the stand, rolling over and drifting off.

Chapter Nine

Andi didn't open her eyes, but knew it was light. Stretching until the tips of her toes touched the foot of the bed, she relished the pleasantness of just lying here, so comfortable, so safe.

Safe? That's strange, she realized. *I don't consider myself fearful or phobic.* A frown erased the little smile she'd known was there, and it stayed, even when she consciously tried to dislodge it. Everything had been so wonderful last evening, even washing all that chicken—especially after Keith came to help.

She'd enjoyed the barbecuing and the dinner with its two desserts, the merry-go-round with its calliope and silly animals, being thrown together during the other ride—even the storm...

She tried to tell herself this latter was responsible for feelings she was having—but didn't believe that.

Opening her eyes, she discovered it was nearly 7:30 in the morning of what must be a beautiful day. The leaves beyond her window looked especially bright and shining, but, going to the window, she saw branches, twigs and leaves scattered over the grass.

Slipping into her lightweight robe, she went to the kitchen. "Good morning!"

Gram was at the stove, stirring something. "And a good morning to you, Annie." Gram moved her pan to a cool burner. "Would you like to share hot cereal cooked with raisins? Or would you prefer something else?"

"Hmmmm." Andi started for the cupboard to get bowls. "I haven't had that kind of hot cereal since Mother made it on cold winter mornings when I was little. I considered it special—not realizing till later that what we ate was often the result of necessity. So yes, I'd love to share it—if there's enough."

"Of course there is. If you didn't want it, I'd put the extra in a container and eat it tomorrow."

"Have you heard anything from Vanessa recently?" Andi asked.

"Funny you should ask. She phoned last evening, looking for Keith." An expression of—was it dismay or simply annoyance with herself?—crossed her face. "But when you came in like drowned rats, I forgot to give the message."

Andi chose to respond to the first part. "We did look pretty bad, didn't we?"

"I'm afraid you did." But then she came back to the call. "She said it was important, that she needed to talk with him. But—" she brightened "—she probably left a message on his answering machine."

Could that be the personal matter about which he had to get up really early on this lovely June Saturday? Andi wondered.

Gram went to the phone and dialed. After a short wait, obviously having connected with the electronic gadget, she said, "Vanessa was looking for you yesterday, Keith. She's undoubtedly reached you by now, but if not, you might want to give her a ring. She sounded falsely chipper to me—but perhaps I'm reading too much into the conversation.

"You don't have to call back. For that matter, I'll be outside picking up branches and willow whips." She finished her message with exaggerated forcefulness. "And you needn't call me 'the old faggot woman,' either!"

"I take it there's some joke connected with that?" Andi said.

Gram chuckled. "From the time he could sit up, Keith loved being read to, and one day when he was in the attic with me, we found some old readers—books once used in a nearby one-room country school.

"One of the stories was about a poor old woman who went out in the woods each day to pick up any sticks she could find. She'd fasten them into bundles, or 'faggots,' then go to the market to sell them and buy ground wheat to make a pancake for her little boy.

"As I recall, the story was woefully long-winded, but I'd singsong her cry. 'Fag-gots! Fag-gots, Someone buy my fag-gots. Make your house all warm and nice, and fill my wee boy's mouth.'

"One day when I was in the yard picking up sticks and branches following a storm, a neighbor dropped by. Three-year-old Keith looked up at him and solemnly announced that I was an old faggot woman."

Andi laughed, and Gram made a face. "That's what the neighbor did—thought it hilarious! But the little guy indignantly informed him that it was *true*. I was an old faggot woman trying to earn money so I could buy him bread to eat!"

"That's delightful." It was endearing to think of this engineer, this fine man, as such an intense little boy.

"He was a darling—still is, for that matter...."

"Do you have other pictures of him as a boy than the one on the piano?"

"Doesn't every grandmother?" The crinkles around the outside of her bright eyes deepened. "Want to see some?"

"Definitely."

Gram glanced out the window as she started for the hallway. "I'd get soaked picking up sticks till things dry off a bit, anyway."

Andi had hardly noticed what turned out to be a two-foot stack of albums at the end of the tall, wide, glass-fronted bookcase in the TV room. Gram moved the lamp from on top of them, folded the embroidered cover, and ran her finger down along the precisely labeled albums. "I won't bother you with all of them, so you say where to begin."

The tip of Andi's tongue circled her lips, and she was aware of an increased heart rate. *I couldn't have hoped for a better opportunity!* she thought. "The oldest ones are on the bottom?"

"The very bottom one is from Phil's mother, and the next I received after my father died."

"Would you—could we look at yours, maybe? The

second from the bottom?'' I must not sound too eager, too curious, she told herself.

"You're sure you want to go back that far?''

"This was your home, right? I'd like to see what it looked like years ago—and you and your family, too.''

Gram carried the volume to the kitchen table, and they sat there going page by page through the visual history of Gram's family. And of mine, Andi reminded herself, though I'm not free to say that. Andi had to clear her throat as she pointed to the likeness of a good-looking, white-haired man. "This is your grandfather?''

A nod. "And Grandma—Katerina was her name— holding my aunt Katherine when she was an infant.''

My great-grandmother and grandmother! Andi almost cried out.

As they turned pages, Gram told about the people and places. She told of the water-run lumber mill her great-grandfather had gone to work in as a boy and of which he eventually became half owner. She sighed. "It's sad, though. The river and creeks were essential to the business, yet it was one of the really big floods that destroyed the mill. And the booms. And everything.''

"The booms?''

"Man-made separate obstacles built in the river. When connected together with chains, fastened to floating logs, they served to catch and hold the other logs floated downstream from where crews cut, trimmed and dragged them.''

"Oh.'' She would definitely come back to this topic later, but right now Andi needed to know something. "What did he do when he no longer had the mill?" Does Dad know this? she wondered. I've asked for information, but he never seemed to have any.

"Well, he owned half the mountainside—which was almost stripped of timber—but he was way ahead of his time in several important ways. He continued paying his workmen to clean up everything at the mill site, and then to replant that mountainside with seedlings.

"He'd already built this house, so the family stayed here—though no longer with servants living on the third floor. And he'd built other houses here and in Dalton—so was able to rent those. And then he got involved with railroads, which were *big* in those days...."

She glanced up at the antique schoolhouse clock between the windows. "Oh, my goodness, Annie, look at the time—11:41!" Gram jumped to her feet. "If it's okay with you, we'll just have toasted cheese sandwiches and tomato soup for lunch, since there's a baked-steak dinner at the fire hall tonight."

"We don't have to toast the sandwiches, Gram."

Gram still fretted. "I never sit like this all morning."

Andi reached for her hand. "I'm pleased you spent this time showing me pictures and telling me about ancestors."

"You must be bored stiff!"

"I assure you, I am not one tiny bit bored." She saw that Gram wasn't convinced. "As God is my witness."

She'd never said that before in her life, and she'd

done it now to reassure this woman she'd come to love. And it does mean something to me, too, she thought, something really special. Something I'm just beginning to know....

The women were in the side yard gathering branches that the storm had blown off the trees, when Keith came striding around the house. "So my grandmother's enlisted a helper!"

Andi was delighted to see him. "You must have listened to your answering machine—"

"—and dashed over to offer assistance," he finished, giving her that wholehearted smile.

"Is Vanessa all right, dear?" Gram asked.

Was there a slight hesitation before his answer? Andi wondered.

"She was upset about several things, but we had a long talk. I think she's okay."

Concern still showed on her face. "I hope so, Keith. Remember, if there's something—anything I can help with, I'm available."

"I know that, Gram." He gave her a brief hug. "She does, too."

He joined them in picking up some of these branches, then went around to the front of the house to drag back two large ones. "Did you hear on the radio—and it will be in the paper—that our town council's authorized trucks to pick up storm-related trash on Monday and Tuesday?"

"Good!" Gram gave a sigh of relief. "Getting rid of this is such a bother! Especially for the older folks."

She doesn't put herself in that category, Andi realized. Will I be this young when I'm in my seventies? This brought Andi to more thoughts she'd seldom entertained. What was age, anyway? A chance to learn more. To share more. To love more—and to be loved.

"I have a confession," Keith said. "I'm here under false pretenses."

Andi cringed inwardly, knowing *she* was the one guilty of this. Nothing he'd "confess" could be greater than her deception. However, she sighed dramatically. "So you didn't really want to help."

"It's worse than that," he admitted cheerfully. "I'm about to ask you to do something for—or with me."

Her head tilted to the side. "It involves chicken-scrubbing?" He shook his head. "Turning grills?"

"There's nothing 'fowl' about this request. Honest." And then he laughed, seeing through her pretend scowl at the awfulness of his play on words. "As you know, the pet parade was scheduled for last night, because that was to be the kickoff, and we need an extra-large turnout on one of the first nights if we're to make this a financial success.

"However, this change complicates a number of other things—one being that Karlyn, who was supposed to be joining me, has a conflict. And Vanessa says she doesn't want to do it."

She almost teased him about being third choice, but instead said, "This sounds like something I shouldn't say yes to till I get details."

Gram nodded firmly. "Smart girl we have here, Keith."

"And pretty, too!"

''So now you're trying to flatter me into agreeing?''

He grinned at her. ''Is it working?''

''You're incorrigible, Keith McHenry!'' She was enjoying this repartee.

''So I've been told.'' But then he explained, ''Dad goes all out with his parade floats, which almost always end up involving our family. His theme this year is 'When the Susquehanna River was Frontier,' with him as an Indian, 'rowing' his canoe down Main Street. I'm to be a settler and *you*, I hope, will be my everlovin' wife and the mother of our Jake and Traci and Brock and Melody.''

''You've got to be kidding!''

''Not in the least. You're a little more slender than Karlyn, I think—'' he gave her a deliberately obvious once-over ''—and will look fantastic wearing the dress Karlyn chose from one of Gram's trunks in the attic—''

''You're in on this, too?'' she challenged Gram.

''Just as wardrobe supplier. They always keep the float a secret, so this is the first I heard what she and Keith were rummaging for up there. And why.''

''Well?'' She studied his face. ''What's involved?''

''There's a log cabin on my woodsy-decorated truck—which is pulling Dad's canoe. You and I and our kids will be walking—barefoot, if you don't object.''

This did sound like fun, she thought, but waited to hear him out. ''I'll have an antique musket over my shoulder and occasionally 'shoot' at deer or maybe at bears, cougars or turkeys in the trees along Main

Street. You'll be carrying an old hoe and perhaps chop every so often at imaginary weeds.

"Three of 'our kids' will be leading their own pet dogs, but Jake has been practicing for at least two weeks with a sheep borrowed from a neighbor."

She gave in easily. "How could I possibly refuse being in such a major production with that stellar a cast?"

"Especially me?" he asked with raised brows.

"*And* the neighbor's sheep...."

She donned the long, pink-and-blue flowered gingham, and went to look in the full-length hall mirror, while adjusting the matching bonnet. "This outfit's so beautiful, Gram! I feel blessed being allowed to wear it."

"I made it at the time of our nation's Bicentennial festivities. In '76." She adjusted the fit over one shoulder. "It's good to see it used again—by you."

If only I could let you know we're family, thought Andi, *you'd be even more pleased at my wearing your handiwork.*

Keith let out a long, low whistle as she descended the staircase to meet him. "I should be taking you somewhere much more grand than walking the streets of Sylvan Falls!"

He looked handsomely rugged in those heavy-duty, gray wool pants and a long-sleeved, open-banded, off-white shirt.

"Ah'm jus' proud to be escorted anywhere by you, my frontier husband."

"You both sound like B movie characters," Gram informed them.

"Sorry we don't have better scriptwriters, Gram," he drawled. "But I do think she looks great."

Andi decided they'd better not tease much more, though he was obviously enjoying it.

"Be sure to look over here on the porch as you go by," Gram reminded as they went outside. "Several from my Sunday School class will be with me, and who knows how many more?"

Keith promised they'd do as requested. Then they headed for his car, parked at the end of the walk, and were off on what Andi regarded as another adventure.

The school parking lot was crowded with floats, parade units, groups and singles, and she felt like a child, reveling in the sights and sounds. Horses, pigs, sheep, donkeys and cows were there, along with the expected cats, dogs and rabbits. Birds of many kinds were in cages: parrots, canaries, pigeons, peacocks, ducks and geese.

"But I don't like snakes." Andi shuddered at seeing a girl with a boa constrictor draped around her shoulders.

"I'm surprised." He was maneuvering to find a place to park. "You seem so with it."

"Sorry to disappoint you, Keith. I can handle frogs and crayfish, ladybugs and worms and spiders, but get chills from snakes."

"Have you ever touched one?"

"*Seeing* them gives me the creeps, so I'm not about to handle them!"

He didn't respond at once, acting as though he'd either not heard or didn't care what she said. But then he suggested, "Sometimes it's better to face our fears and uncertainties. No matter how hard that is."

Is he lecturing me? About snakes? He glanced her way, probably aware of her studying his profile. His little smile, a slight upturn at the corners of his mouth, didn't quite reach his eyes as he covered her ringless hand lying on her lap. "My apologies, Annie. That was uncalled for—a leftover bit of advice from speaking with someone else today, concerning something quite removed from reptiles."

Her hand turned beneath his, their fingers intertwining for a moment before his returned to the steering wheel. He parked in a space so small that she wouldn't even have considered it.

He was talking with Vanessa today, she thought. About something more serious than he wanted Gram to know.

They got out of the car and, holding hands to keep from being separated, hurried to find Zack and his float. On the way, they spoke with people about animals, music groups, costumes and this wonderful weather.

Zack was in his glory, happily giving instructions and directing his "actors" as to their historical presentation.

To Andi, everything had seemed bedlam. "How do they do it—get everyone whipped into shape like this?" she asked five minutes before the Sylvan Falls school band was scheduled to start the parade.

"I don't have a clue, Annie. Even after living here all my life and being in the parades almost every year, I'm still amazed that it always gets pulled off."

"You're not personally involved with organizing this?"

"Others seem to have the gift for doing it, and *I'm* here to enjoy myself."

Andi had noticed at Karlyn's how tanned Zack was for this early in the season. With his black hair and muscular body, he could almost pass for a native Indian as he knelt in the canoe centered on a child's large wagon, cardboard wavelets camouflaging whatever was necessary to make it secure.

"That man driving the truck—is he a relative?"

"That's Uncle Brad. You didn't meet him, did you?"

She hadn't noticed him in the crowd, nor seen him climb into the cab, but he was sitting tall, so was probably as big as Keith. He seemed to be enjoying himself in the role of driver.

Just because he's without a job, Andi told herself, and his daughter's having problems, doesn't mean he shouldn't have a good time. Or that he doesn't have a pleasant disposition.

Andi always went to concerts early, to be there when musicians started tuning instruments; the excitement of these bands and participants was equally contagious.

Impatience. Nervousness. A horse pulling out of line and being reined in. One child, then another, starting to cry, and a third throwing himself onto the macadam in a temper tantrum. Volunteers walking along the extended line, giving instructions and encouragement, cheering people on.

Right on time, the fire siren sounded and the fire chief's car moved forward. The color guard and school band, in perfect formation and with invigorating marching music, followed him. Then a scout troop from town, and the first six high-stepping horses…on and on they went.

"You kids have been wonderfully patient with all this waiting," Andi complimented, as Brad started the motor and inched the truck forward, into the parade. "The rest of this evening is going to be sheer delight!"

And that began almost immediately for her. She'd hugged each child before looking up at Keith, wanting to share her sense of expectation, but the expression she saw on his face, in his eyes, was of pure joy.

Chapter Ten

Andi walked beside him, the children sometimes ahead and sometimes behind or off to the side, depending more on the whims of the pets than on their handlers' control.

Melody, Evelyn's four-year-old who'd chosen the old collie, had the least difficulty. At least three times her age, the dog was content doing anything her mistress desired.

Brock had insisted on bringing the young beagle which, as his father said last Sunday, "...shows promise of becoming a good hunter, but hasn't yet given up wanting to do things *his* way."

Traci was struggling with all her five-year-old's determination to lead the middle-aged, short-haired dachshund. Andi would have liked to help more, but Traci informed her, "I want to do it my *own* self." The child did, however, accept Keith's assistance several times.

Jake started out well with the borrowed, full-grown

sheep, but was mortified when, in front of Gram's, it decided to go no farther. Keith did no more "shooting bear or turkeys" until he helped get the recalcitrant animal on the go again. Other people's pets didn't always do as desired, either—which added to the enjoyment of the crowds lining the streets.

Andi had never craved the spotlight except when in plays and musicals at school, so at first felt ill at ease in her role as a frontier woman. However, she was soon enjoying her pretend weed-chopping, helping the children—and walking, barefoot, side-by-side with Keith.

He must be as highly regarded—as evidenced by his being called by onlookers—as his father. She'd presumed Zack was representing a stereotypical Indian, but in broken English he identified himself as *Shickellamy.*

"Shicke-*what?*" she asked.

"Shick*ellamy.*" Keith emphasized the last syllables. "One of the greatest of all Indian statesmen. Sent down from the Five Nations of Indians, in New York, to make and keep peace throughout all of central Pennsylvania."

"What an awesome responsibility! Did he do it?"

"He excelled in every way. Had he lived longer— he and Conrad Weiser, the official interpreter for the colonists—we might not have gone through those horrible uprisings and massacres of the French and Indian and Revolutionary Wars."

"I'm terribly weak where history's concerned."

"Ask Dad. He'll love telling you about it." He grinned. "In great detail, I must warn you. He belongs to three historical societies and has a huge li-

brary and prefers reading history tomes to watching
football.''

Amazing, she thought. Here he is, a mechanic—
but so much more! He owns his dealership and garage, is a community leader and history buff—and
who knows what else? A good son and father and
grandfather, that's for sure, and a loving husband and
church worker... As for me, I don't even know my
family history. And I should know Dad better—I
should ask questions....

"Something bothering you, Annie?"

She was startled from her reverie and responded
without considering consequences. "I was thinking
about your father, Keith. And mine."

"Tell me about yours."

She looked around, seeking a way out of the opening she'd given him—and was grateful for the excuse
of walking over to help Jake get his sheep moving
forward again. Melody had kept up with them all this
while, but now complained of being tired. Andi
picked her up, set her in the canoe with Zack, and
took over leading the collie.

As she should have expected, Traci immediately
became "tired" also, as did the boys. It took Andi,
Keith and Zack to coax and cajole them into walking
the short distance from there to the carnival grounds,
where their mothers would pick them up.

Each participant was given a free ticket by the firemen, so they—in addition to all the people having
come specifically for rides—formed long lines at the
Ferris wheel and other amusements. Gram met Andi
to take her in to the baked-steak dinner, but Keith

said he could join them if they'd wait fifteen or twenty minutes.

"The last time you told me that here," Gram reminded, "you never did eat."

"I remember." He rolled his eyes. "It was Roy Gage's barn that burned...."

Sliding into her shoes, Andi did not enter this conversation, though she hoped he'd eat with them. Gram, obviously desiring that too, said they'd get in line to buy three tickets, and he should come right to the table.

Vanessa was with him when he arrived. "Hi, Gram. And Annie, it was nice of you to fill in on such short notice."

"I enjoyed it," Andi replied sincerely. "I've never done anything like this before."

"You seemed to be having fun. And that outfit's lovely on you."

Andi was surprised at the compliment, but it seemed heartfelt. Vanessa was probably very sweet once you got to know her. Andi realized that Vanessa's astounding good looks probably intimidated people—especially other women. Did she fall into that category as well? Andi resolved to be more friendly to Vanessa. After all, Keith seemed to think highly of his cousin, and that was good enough for Andi.

"Gram did a great job—material, pattern, everything."

Andi started to push back her chair. "We didn't see you, Vanessa, so saved only the one seat. I'll move over there—" she indicated a single on the far side of the table, eight places down "—so you can all be together."

Gram snorted. "You'll do no such thing!"

Keith's foot blocked the backward movement of her chair legs. "It's okay, Annie, we'll just—"

The man across from them settled the matter. "Wait a minute, Keith, till me and my missus eat our last bites of pie and empty our coffee cups. Then you two can sit here."

The baked steak was tender and juicy, scalloped potatoes perfect, and vegetables not overdone—which Andi learned was difficult to accomplish when cooking for hundreds of people. However, this meal was not as relaxed and easy as the previous one.

"You look pale, Vanessa. Are you feeling well?" her grandmother asked.

"I'm fine, Gram. I've been awfully busy and haven't had time to lie in the sun."

"You may have to take time, dear. Like last Sunday—maybe you should have gone swimming or something."

Andi didn't know Vanessa well enough to read her expression, but was almost sure she saw tension—and sadness. She felt sympathy for her, and changed the subject. "I understand you're an executive secretary. Do you have an opportunity to use much of your computer background?"

"Definitely!" Vanessa leaned back in her seat. "In working with people all over the world, dealing with problems they're having or improvements and updates they're considering, I'm grateful for every single course I took in college, and for all my experience."

"There's so much to keep up with!" Andi agreed. "With all that's happening in the field, there are times I feel like a computer illiterate!"

Keith got into this, too, speaking of how invaluable computers were with his planning, designing and bidding on building projects. Gram looked from one to another, probably understanding only a fraction of what was said.

For once, Andi made little effort to include her in the conversation, so apologized as they walked home together through the soft pleasantness of this summer evening. "I didn't mean to be rude, Gram, but Vanessa seemed so uncomfortable there at first. Once we started talking about her work and computers, though, she relaxed."

"What makes me so upset is that she has everything going for her. She's beautiful—at least I think so...."

"She is. Very."

"And she's so smart—graduated *summa cum laude* from Penn State, with a three-point-nine average."

"That's impressive."

"And she's always so popular. I don't understand it. She's had some really fine men who loved her, but always seems to pick the wrong ones. I worry about her so much. I know something's wrong, but she won't confide in me. I wish I could help her."

It was a cry of anguish, of love. "I don't know, Gram. I wish I did. I have friends right now who are doing the same thing. They claim to be happy and fulfilled, but..."

Gram may not have even heard her words. "I know I'm getting old. Perhaps I *don't* relate to the world of today—which is what Vanessa said when I brought it up once.''

Andi's hand on her arm was meant to show support as they talked about the problem. As Gram saw it, the one good thing was that Keith had a ''steady head'' on his shoulders. ''Apparently Vanessa confides in him.''

Saying she needed to pick up a prescription, Gram walked on, and Andi went inside. In the kitchen, holding a glass of water, she stared at the phone a while ʹefore picking it up and punching in the numbers. ''Hi, Keith, it's Annie. Is Vanessa there?'' That sounded abrupt, she realized, but she wasn't sure how much time she had.

''No, she's not. Did you want to talk with her?''

''It's you I thought I should perhaps say something to—and I have only a few minutes, since Gram went to the pharmacy. But I'm not trying to interfere or anything.''

''I'm sure you're not.''

She shared the conversation she'd just had, emphasizing Gram's genuine concern. ''Could you perhaps give Gram reassurance—though I can't imagine how that can be done without her guessing I've talked with you.''

''Annie?'' Her name was stretched out, his voice deeper.

''Yes?''

''I do appreciate your calling....''

He seemed about to add more, but didn't. ''But?''

''But,'' he repeated, ''I doubt we'll have time to go into this on the phone. Would you come here? To my home?''

She'd not considered that. "I don't know if..."

"You're questioning my...intentions?" His tone became lighter. "I've got my right hand up in the air and I'm solemnly affirming that I'll behave myself—at least as much as you want me to."

"You're really something, Keith McHenry." She laughed aloud. "How can I explain to Gram that this maiden lady from Chicago is about to go visit her beloved grandson in his mansion and isn't inviting her along as chaperon?"

"I have faith in your coming up with a suitable explanation. You can always tell her you're coming to see my chestnut staircase."

"Wow! What more could a girl ask for?"

She was still smiling when telling Gram that she was going over to Keith's to see the staircase. His grandmother's face lit up. "Oh, I think I—" the sentence became subdued "—will go on to bed. I'm pretty tired."

Andi went along with that. "You've had a busy week. I don't plan to stay long—and I'll try to be quiet when I get back, so I won't wake you."

Gram had started up the stairs before Andi called a goodnight and went outside. The calliope and other music and sounds were far enough away that they were a fairy background for the whispering of leaves in the gentle breeze. This was her first walk after dark on the streets of Sylvan Falls, and she found it peaceful, idyllic. The direct light from street lamps at the intersection was filtered through leaves here on the sidewalk.

She liked the feel of the long gown she'd worn as wife of the rugged frontiersman and as mother to their

four beautiful children—and was almost overwhelmed by an unexpected longing, by desire. What
would it be like to come to Keith as his wife? To live
with him in the big, white, German-sided house only
a few steps away?

She'd half expected that he'd be waiting on the
porch, but he was not. She raised her hand to ring the
bell, but the door opened, and he was there.

Andi walked inside—and into his arms, hers holding him as tightly as his were around her.

No words were spoken, none needed. Her face was
buried against his shoulder and neck, his cheek
against her hair.

So this is what it's like to come home to Keith, she
thought. She had no idea how long they remained like
that. It was she who finally forced herself to draw
away, and he permitted that, moving his hands slowly
down her arms, taking her hands in his.

Her head tilted forward. She must not look long
into those beautiful brown eyes that could be so trans-
parent, could show such tenderness. "I'm sorry...."

"I will never regret your coming tonight." His
voice was soft. "My holding you...."

How could I have let this happen? Andi asked herself. What have I done?

Shifting both slender hands into his bigger, stronger
left one, he lifted her chin with a forefinger. "Look
at me, Annie. Please."

"I'm—ashamed. I didn't mean to act like some
flighty little teenager."

"It's all right, dear. Don't be afraid."

She did look into his eyes and, even in the poorly
lit hallway, saw that smile, that joy she'd seen earlier.

"I should not have come." She started to pull away and, almost surprisingly, he let her do so.

Her leg almost gave way as she turned suddenly, preparing to leave, and he reached to steady her. "Annie?"

She stood there, confused. He said, "You came to talk with me, remember? If I promise to do nothing more to frighten you, will you please come into the sitting room?"

It's not you that I don't trust, Andi thought. *I had no idea I was this vulnerable—that in one short week I could fall in love! In love with a man there's no chance of my marrying.... And I've been completely dishonest with you!*

Andi scarcely paid attention to the pieces of obviously antique furniture in the large, white-walled room. Books and papers were scattered over the couch, but she wouldn't have sat there anyway. Instead, she chose a small, low rocker; no matter where he sat, they'd be separated by an arm's length.

He appeared fairly relaxed in his heavily-carved, high-backed armchair. "Thank you for coming."

"I love Gram, Keith." *Even saying her name, and yours, gives me pleasure.*

"Me, too."

"I know. It hurts to see her so concerned about Vanessa. And she's worried about Brad—"

"She may have the right to be." He drew in a deep breath. "You no doubt know that Aunt Paula's a brilliant trial lawyer. All of us are proud of her. The problem is, she's driven by her need for excellence—and recognition. I suppose she always has been, though in the early days we considered that admirable.''

He drew in a deep breath. "There was never a question about Uncle Brad's dropping out of the university in order to see her started in law school and on her way. But when it should have been *his* turn, as had been agreed, she wouldn't—perhaps couldn't, I don't know—give up anything to make that happen.

"Gram even offered to mortgage her house, to borrow the money to see him through—he's every bit as brilliant as his wife, by the way. But that was rejected, by both of them.

"Then Vanessa came along." He leaned forward, elbows on his knees. "According to pictures, she wasn't beautiful as a baby, though I don't remember. She was sickly, crying constantly and not sleeping. Professional child care wasn't working, so Uncle Brad quit his job to care for her.

"He did his best, but Aunt Paula blamed him for their daughter's failure to thrive." He paused, perhaps waiting for Andi to say something. "Gram, Mom and Aunt Phyllis all tried to help, but were informed they were 'spoiling' her—that they were part of the problem."

"That must have been very difficult."

"Some of that's carried over to this day," he admitted. "My aunt and uncle are always invited to family affairs, but Paula's usually 'too busy' to attend. Once Van stopped living with her parents, she began coming, though. Unfortunately, she can't talk with them about much of anything—yet Aunt Paula still influences her too much."

"And her father?"

"He's well-liked and apparently had little trouble finding work, once Van went to school full-time. But it was low paying—at least compared with hers—therefore of less importance. Or worth."

"That's sad!"

He leaned his head back against the chair, brow furrowed. "I can't imagine forcing myself to get up in the morning, to shower, shave, get dressed, eat—then drive to a job I hate. Or am ashamed of. Day after day. Month after month—"

"So he quit?"

Keith nodded. "He'd been conscientious and hard-working, and felt like a quitter at first. But as one job followed another, he waited less and less time before handing in his resignation, storming out or getting fired.

"And his wife's become increasingly less sympathetic." Keith's right hand pushed back through his hair. "Van's always felt caught in the middle—convinced she's the cause of the dysfunction in their family. And in their relationship to our extended family."

"That's an awful burden for a child. *And* for an adult." Was this why she'd experienced that moment of pity?

A frown was on his face, hesitancy in his manner. "What I'm about to tell you has been a closely guarded secret."

She slid to the edge of her seat, stretching to place a hand on his knee—but stopped in time. "It's best not to share it then. You'll be sorry, come morning."

He'd seen her almost-touch, but probably because of his promise not to upset her, withdrew the hand that had moved toward hers. "I'm convinced you're trustworthy, Annie."

She straightened, no longer meeting his gaze. *And I can't even be open enough to tell you my real name!* she thought guiltily.

"I know a secret's not a secret when once told, but I'll just say that she's had many disappointing relationships with men. She always seems to be attracted to the wrong kind of guy. Despite her beauty and brains, she doesn't have a lot of confidence. She's just managed to break off another bad relationship. I'm trying to help her. It's a rough time, and I hope she doesn't go back to the guy."

"So she's lonely?"

"Very."

"If I were staying longer," she said softly, "I would try to be a friend to her."

"That could be another good reason for my wishing you wouldn't leave soon."

She couldn't permit herself to pick up on those softly spoken words. "What about her family? Can't they help?"

"Aunt Paula's a workaholic. She's never been there much for Van. Uncle Brad has, probably from frustration and poor self-esteem, been coping less and less well with life. I know for a fact that he didn't just 'leave' his last couple of jobs—he was fired. For poor performance."

"Which doesn't help his self-esteem, does it?"

"Right! So Van's concerned about that, too, especially with his drinking."

"Oh."

"She thinks that's why he doesn't come to family

things." When she nodded, he went on. "As far as she knows, he's not *driving* when under the influence—Aunt Paula's threatened to leave, and to take everything if he does."

They stumbled through several other topics before arriving at the far more pleasant one of today's parade and things his nieces and nephews said and did.

It wasn't long before she reminded him to show her his staircase, and she agreed that whoever had applied paint to all this chestnut woodwork should have his head examined.

She commended him for the good job he was doing, but begged off when he offered to show her the rest of the house. "Though I'm sure it will be even more lovely than Gram's when it's finished."

"If I live long enough to do all that's needed!"

Andi had felt secure when coming alone, but didn't argue when he announced he was walking her home. There was only a handclasp at the door, then he asked, "Do you mind if I come for breakfast in the morning? As usual?"

"Of course you'll come! Gram will be disappointed if you aren't here."

"And you?"

She didn't answer. "I'll be ready for breakfast and to go to Sunday School and church."

His smile looked perfectly normal—and *perfect* did seem to be the right word. "Sleep well, Annie."

"You too, Keith. And thanks for a wonderful day—from faggot-collecting to marching with 'our' kids—" glancing down at the gown she was wearing "—to baked steak, and chestnut staircases."

"You're easy to please, Annie."

"Is that good?"

"With you, it is. And I must also add that you please easily."

"Playing on words?"

"No, Annie—making a statement." He gave a small bow, turned and, with a wave of his arm, ran down the steps.

Chapter Eleven

She locked the door and turned off the porch and TV-room lights before taking off her shoes to tiptoe up the stairs. A sliver of light showed beneath Gram's door, but Andi went to her own room for pajamas and slippers before heading for the bathroom.

The warm sudsy water was soothing, and by the time she got out of the tub she had no doubt that she'd be asleep shortly. She started to read another chapter, but laid it back on the stand, telling herself *today* was better than a dozen books.

She must call Dad tomorrow; he'd be wondering how things were going. She'd brought her laptop, thinking she'd make notes, but each person was so *real*, such a separate entity, that she'd never forget nor get them mixed up.

I'm already thinking of them in the past, she thought—and was appalled! I don't want to leave them forever—there has to be some other way....

She turned and tossed, trying to figure things out....

She had loved Jon as a wonderful friend, and they'd been almost as close as siblings—at least that's what she'd thought.

But here she'd discovered a different kind of tie—the kind that made Karlyn knock herself out having innumerable family get-togethers in addition to being a dedicated single mother, full-time teacher, Sunday School teacher—and who knew what else?

Keith. How wonderful he was! Everyone liked and respected him. A genuinely good man, she thought, giving of himself so generously—asking so little in return. He loves his family, his town—and may be starting to love me, too. If so, I'm being unfair, perhaps cruel—to let him do so.

And Gram—so concerned for family that she offered to mortgage her home to help her son complete his education. She loved her husband so much that she continued the work she'd done with him in the fire company even years after he died.

And taking strangers—like Andi—into her house.

And I'm repaying that by deceiving her! Andi thought. She was so agitated that she actually punched her pillow. Then, realizing the futility of her action, she rolled over, trying to find a comfortable position.

It's not my physical body causing discomfort right now, she finally admitted silently. It's my mind. My conscience. My soul.

Her eyes flew open and she stared at a window, a rectangle of only slight illumination. She sensed leaves on the tree, but couldn't make out a single, individual one.

It's like that with my mind, she thought. She tried

to keep from considering the rest of her previous thought. *Conscience* was bad enough, but *soul?*

What was *happening* to her in Sylvan Falls?

She turned on the bedside light and tried to get interested in *Aikenside,* but after the third page admitted she had no recollection of what her eyes had seen.

Getting up and walking around didn't help, either. On top of the second dresser was a set of heavy bookends with embossed angels holding bouquets of violets. A Bible was between them, along with a volume of daily meditations. Picking up the latter, dated two years earlier, she absently riffled pages until she got to this date.

The heading was Compassion, which she didn't think she needed right now. Or did she?

With a sigh, she carried it to the little rocker she'd sat in during her first night here. Maybe God wants to give me a message, she thought—and almost returned the book.

A half-smile flitted across her face. Just because last week's Sunday School lesson had been so applicable didn't mean that she need expect to have messages plunked in her path again!

She found nothing especially inspiring or helpful for herself in these words, nor in the verse of scripture at the beginning, nor the prayer at the end—not even in the suggested passage she forced herself to look up in the Bible.

So what did I expect? she asked herself, replacing both books between the bookends. Turning, she glanced at the clock: 12:09. And she was still wide awake....

She was sitting on the side of the bed when it hit her—this was a new day, *not* the date she'd looked up! She went and brought the volumes back again.

The portion she'd read was on the right-hand page—and she almost held her breath as she turned to the next one. Her fingertips touched the word at the top, passing slowly across it as though it were written in Braille.

Integrity! She was almost afraid to read what was written—she even started to close the book.

Uncanny. Incredible. Unexplainable.

It was a first-person account about the time, as a teen, that the writer's father took her along when buying lumber to build a back porch. Boards were counted out and put in the truck and the bill calculated. Dad stopped in the process of writing his check, however, to ask the owner to refigure the cost. Looking annoyed, the man finally did as requested—and found he'd undercharged by over a third!

On the way home, the daughter burst out, "You didn't have to tell him, Dad! He'd never have known!"

Her father replied, "But *I* would have, and so would God. There's not enough building material in that whole yard to tempt me to break my relationship with God."

I didn't understand, and I thought of what I could have done with all that money he'd thrown away. But then I began noting other things about my dad—how hard he worked, how disciplined he was, how he always did what he said he was going to, how he tithed—and how he loved Mom and my brother and me. And God.

And I became very proud of this man who never got to college, nor made a lot of money, nor became well known in the world. But what he does have is an incorruptible adherence to the teachings of God, and these morals and ethics have been passed on to my generation and to the next.

Thanks, Dad, for showing me what it means to be a Christian.

And thank *you*, God, for him.

What has this got to do with me? Andi wondered. I'm not cheating anyone—I'm trying to decide how much to *give* them, not how to take anything away.

Integrity. Ethics. Morals. Muddled together in her head. She went back to bed, but did not sleep for a long time. When she finally did, there were dreams.

And then there was the siren blaring! Oh, God, please help the firemen. Help Keith! Please keep him safe.... It didn't seem incongruous to ask for favors; it seemed right.

There was movement in the hall. Andi went to the door and saw Gram starting down the stairs, looking troubled, though her voice sounded normal. "I'm going down to make a pot of tea."

"May I come, too?"

"Of course." So they went together, both knowing that tea wasn't what they needed.

"I suppose Keith will be..." Andi started, but couldn't even guess what he'd be doing.

"He's a good boy." Gram turned on the scanner

as soon as they got to the kitchen. The first report concerned an ambulance call in Dalton, but then the commands and instructions of personnel here in Sylvan Falls were coming fast—and it was Keith's voice giving precise directions to the farm, where a cattle barn was burning.

Reports from the site. Cows being taken out. A young stallion so scared it reared up, his flailing hooves injuring someone, perhaps seriously. An ambulance on its way. Keith again, voice calm.

Tea steeped in its pot, mugs waited on the table. The women talked little, and Gram was sitting there, unmoving.

"May I pour your tea, Gram?"

"Yes, dear. Thanks."

"Gram?"

Her shoulders and head turned, Gram's neck probably stiff from tension. "What is it, Annie?"

"Is there anything we can do?"

"We can pray."

And they did, sometimes with mug in hand, other times while the scanner squawked communications from emergency headquarters.

Pulling in volunteer fire companies from two nearby communities.

The firefighters tried to save outbuildings—the corncrib already in flames, but perhaps the others…

"At least we had that rain, the night before last," Gram said. "Things were awfully dry before that."

A firefighter hurt—no name or condition given. Gram looked almost ill, and Andi knew she must be reliving the death of her beloved Phil. In how many homes were people sitting or lying or pacing as they prayed for loved ones?

An hour passed. Another. An accident in Dalton and a break-in were given precedence over the barn fire, which they could only hope was being brought under control.

The first company called in from a nearby town was finally leaving. Eventually, the one from the second community was excused.

What of the two injured people? Andi wondered desperately. Who were they? How badly were they hurt?

Leftover tea was poured into a large Pyrex cup and reheated in the microwave. They drank some of it.

I'm glad I'm still here, for Gram's sake, she thought. Does she get up every time this happens at night? It didn't seem appropriate to ask that now. "Gram, Keith said he'll be here for breakfast."

"Keith—I love him so much!" Gram was staring into the darkness outside one of the back windows.

Andi felt the same, but dared not say the words aloud. Besides, she had to get Gram thinking of something other than those fighting that fire. "What will you have for breakfast, since Keith's coming?" As if that mattered!

Gram blinked a couple times, focusing on Andi. "I—planned for buckwheat cakes and liverwurst. I bought the liverwurst yesterday, because he likes it so much."

"*Liverwurst?* Like in sandwiches?"

She shook her head. "We have a country store with an excellent meat department. They process their own liverwurst—with seasonings almost exactly like the old German farmers around here have done for generations."

Andi got Gram talking about her childhood here in Sylvan Falls, and Gram went to the other room and brought back the old picture album. Her grandfather looked stiffly formal, sitting on an ornately carved wooden chair with Katerina, his wife, standing behind but to the side, probably to show her full-skirted, tight-bodiced, high-necked black dress.

Gram said they'd been well-respected, but, as she recalled, her grandparents never smiled. "And by then they'd been through a lot with their daughter."

"What happened?" This would be Dad's mother, about whom she remembered far too little, though Katherine had lived with them a while before she died.

"I don't know exactly—not everything. She was quite beautiful...."

Yes, my memories and the few pictures I've seen of Katherine indicate that to be true. "The other day you showed me one of her as a baby. Are there more?"

Gram turned some pages. "Ah, here she is—her high school graduation picture. She's pretty, isn't she?"

Katherine was looking into the camera, a pensive expression on her face. "Yes, she is. And she'd be even more attractive if her hair wasn't pulled back so severely and she wasn't so—stiff. And I wish she was wearing something more becoming than that high-necked, plain dress."

"I agree."

"She seems sad, somehow."

Gram drew in a deep breath. "I never met her, so all I know is what Dad told me. He was about fifteen when she was born, so was probably more uncle-ish than brother-ish—if there are such words. He adored her—wanted to do all kinds of things for her, but that wasn't allowed."

"Not allowed?"

"My grandparents were extremely 'religious'—in the strictest sense. In church at least twice on Sunday and on Wednesday night for sure. Not only was cleanliness next to godliness, but plainness and seriousness, as well.

"Dad insisted that if he or Katherine did anything wrong, they were prayed over for hours at a time. And they almost never ate a hot meal, for the gravy and mashed potatoes congealed on the table while chapters were read from the Bible and lengthy prayers were said."

She sighed, hand turning a page. "Dad didn't rebel, but left home when he was seventeen, putting himself through college by working weekends, evenings and holidays. His folks never did approve—couldn't understand wanting an education, let alone becoming an educator.

"Did I tell you he was principal of Dalton High for over thirty years?"

"That's impressive." But she had to learn more about her grandmother. "Did he—see Katherine much?"

Her head moved from left to right. "Dad wasn't welcome at the farm—was told that he was 'a bad influence' on his sister. He did go see her here at school, sometimes, till word got back to their father, who threatened to get a restraining order if he did it again.... So Dad decided to wait till she graduated, then bring her into his home—*our* home, since I was a child then.

"But one week after graduation, she disappeared."

"Disappeared?" She was sounding like a parrot, repeating Gram's words. "Where did she go?"

"He never knew. Exactly. Grampa blamed *him* for putting crazy ideas in her head—perhaps even helping her get away. I know Katherine took money, maybe a couple of hundred dollars, and left a note saying she didn't consider this stealing, and that they shouldn't either."

"It sounds like she admitted taking it."

"*She* felt she'd earned it, having helped on the farm with harvesting, taking care of cows and chickens, canning, freezing, making hay, just about everything—and never being paid.

"*His* idea was that he'd fed and clothed her all these years and saw to it she got a 'proper upbringing,' whatever that is. Now, when she'd graduated from school and could be around all the time to earn her keep, she'd run away."

"She never got in touch? Didn't write or call or anything?" This doesn't seem like the wonderful grandmother I remember, Andi thought.

"She wrote at least twice—her letters are in the old family Bible I brought here when Dad died."

"May I see them?" Andi thrust her hands under the edge of the table to keep Gram from seeing them shake. After all these years—a contact with Katherine! She must calm down—make this a *normal* request. "This is such a great story, Gram. You've made Katherine so real that I'd love to see her letters, if you wouldn't mind.''

Gram looked from her to the windows and back again, smile slightly twisted. ''Annie, you are a marvel!''

Has she seen through me? Andi wondered worriedly. My interest in Katherine?

Before she decided how to respond, Gram explained, ''It will soon be full light. Morning. You've kept me company through this whole night—kept me from worrying myself sick over which firefighters were hurt—and how badly. And you've kept me talking—about lots of things, but mostly about my family, people you've never known. You can't be interested in all this!''

''You couldn't be more wrong, Gram. I am very interested in your father. And his sister. And I *would* like to see Katherine's letters.'' *Oh, God, please,* she found herself praying, *when I'm this close, don't let me lose the opportunity.*

''Well, if you're sure....'' She got up stiffly from the kitchen chair, and Andi followed her into the parlor, the large room to the right when entering from the porch. She had looked in here many times, admiring the massive Victorian couch and chairs, the teak and mahogany tables, Oriental carpet, objets d'art and, especially, the big mahogany desk with its tall, leaded-glass bookcase.

Going to the stand under one of the windows, Gram picked up a heavy, tooled-leather Bible, sat down and slid back on the couch, laying the volume on her lap. She opened it at the section between the Old and New Testaments.

"Just look at that artwork!" Andi exclaimed. "The brilliance of the coloring! It looks like that done during the Middle Ages."

Gram smiled. "It's not *that* old, but it's been in our family for hundreds of years. I treasure it."

"I'm glad you do." What an understatement! Andi wanted to cry. What a wealth of information there is here—all these generations! She tried to be calm as Gram turned several more pages.

"Here we are. Katherine Elizabeth, see? Here's the record of her birth, right after my father's."

"Yes, I do see. Do your children have copies of this?"

"Oh, goodness, no!" She laughed. "None of them seem at all interested in ancient history."

"Do they...*know* about Katherine?"

"Of course." She'd answered brusquely, but then a frown appeared. "I must have mentioned to them about her going away like that."

Andi was reminded of the reason for their being in the parlor with the family Bible. "Her letters are here?"

"Right before Matthew, where Dad put them long ago."

Andi gently unfolded the first one, afraid the paper would be brittle with age. It was written on June the twelfth, over a half-century ago!

Dear Michael,
My precious big brother who tried so hard to be my champion and friend, I do thank you! I know what I'm about to do will cause you pain, but I have to leave. I feel as though I'm drying up here

on the farm, as though I'm dying—and I'm too young to die.

Father will be furious when he finds I'm gone. I have no money of my own—never have had— so I'm taking what I can find here this morning. I cannot stay for even one more day in this house, which has become a jail, a penance— though I don't know what I could have done to earn such punishment.

Yes, I know where I'm going, but can't tell you. Not now. You must be able to say with complete honesty that you had nothing to do with my decision. Or my actions.

I do love you, big brother; it feels wonderful to be free to tell you so. Remember when I put my arms around you and kissed you when I was a little girl of five or six? Did you know Father beat me for that after you were gone? Hugging a man was wanton, he told me. Kissing a man was wicked, and if ever I did it again, I would surely go to hell.

Did you wonder why your little sister no longer came running to you as she had before? It was partly for fear of going to hell, I must admit, for Father's very good at telling of those horrors. But mostly it was fear of him. He could have locked me in my room each time you came, as he'd already done, "for the good of my immortal soul."

I could not bear your being forbidden to come at all!

Only God knows if I can ever have a normal life somewhere far away—but it can't happen here. Pray for me, dear Michael, please pray for me—as I shall pray for you each day of my life.

Someday I'll write and let you know where I am and what I'm doing. My deepest longing is to grow emotionally and psychologically— which is what you, too, must feel I desperately need.

And yes, "desperately" *is* the right word.

With all my love, dear brother, and with thanks for your wanting to help me, I am and ever will be your adoring sister.

                                             Katherine

Andi scanned it first, then reread slowly, carefully. "Where was her mother while this was going on?"

"Totally intimidated, I guess. Maybe it was a male ego thing with the man, I don't know—but Dad said *he* didn't have to put up with this much emotional garbage. Personally, that is—not while he still lived with them.

"But once Katherine left, he made less effort to keep in touch. And they made none to communicate with him."

"What—happened to them?"

"Grandmother died maybe six or eight months after Katherine left—yes, here it is." Her finger pointed to the neatly written information. "Let's see—seven months and nine days. Dad was convinced she just stopped making the effort to live.

"He went to the funeral, in the church they'd always attended. He said he wouldn't have recognized her—skin and bones. Sunken eyes. Yellow-gray skin.

He wondered if she'd eaten anything from the time her daughter left."

"And...her husband?"

"Just sat there, saying nothing. To anyone. And by that time next year, he was gone, too."

Andi stared at her, horrified. "How did Michael bear all this?"

"I've asked myself that, and came to the conclusion he was somehow able to put the whole thing behind him. Which wasn't easy. For one thing, the old man's will stated that he'd disinherited his son and daughter for 'their many sins committed against the saints and against God.'

"His farm and all possessions were left to his church—but the people did let Dad go in and remove pictures, this Bible, and a few other books, and an unopened letter—this one," she said, taking an envelope from the Bible and handing it to Andi.

She slowly removed the single sheet of paper from its yellowed envelope, almost afraid to unfold it again as it had obviously been handled many times. She recognized Katherine's slanting penmanship, but the smudges that looked as though they were from wetness—were they from tears? If so, would they have been hers or her brother's?

Dear Mother and Father,
I hope all is well with you. This last year has been very difficult for me, in many ways—but I am growing.

I have made a wonderful discovery, which I must share with you. I've found a friend, who has been all-important in my finding out who I am and why I'm the way I am. He has been teaching me that I am worthy of being loved— and I've come to love him with all my heart and soul and mind—for that is how he loves me.

I know you've read about him in the four special, wonderful books that I thought I knew very well—Matthew, Mark, Luke, and John. But now I'm reading them with eyes of love—and I'd like so very much if you, too, would read them with open minds and get past all the negatives that have hedged in your hearts.

Please open yourselves to the God of Love. Jesus the Messiah, who wants us all to love, not fear him, is waiting to show you the way.

I pray you will get to really know and love my friend. Maybe then, some day, you can love me, too.

                              Your daughter, Katherine

"Oh, Gram!" There were tears in Andi's eyes. "And her parents never opened it!"

"But my father did. And he immediately sent a letter to the post office box in Lansing, Michigan, which you'll see on the top left corner of that envelope.

"But it came back. There was no way of forwarding it. So he went out there and made all kinds of enquiries, and even hired a well-known agency that specialized in finding missing people, but the investigators drew a blank."

She sighed. "That was the greatest disappointment of his entire life, and he never got over it. Even when he was dying, he called her name."

"You think—" Andi hoped this is what Gram meant "—maybe he *saw* her there, as he was dying?"

There was a pause of several heartbeats before she said, voice hardly audible, "It pleases me to think he did. He met death with a smile on his face, so yes, I'm convinced she was there to greet him."

"How they must have run to hug and to kiss," Andi whispered, tears running down her cheeks, "with never a thought of 'wantonness'—just love."

Chapter Twelve

Gram had gone upstairs, but Andi was still in the parlor when she heard the back door open and the now-familiar, deep voice call, "I'm back!"

Andi was crying and laughing at the same time as she ran through the hallway and kitchen and into his arms. "Keith—oh, Keith, you're all right!"

"Almost, Annie. But utterly exhausted. And *filthy*. You shouldn't even be touching me," he gently scolded. Yet he returned her hug with a fierce embrace, his sooty cheek pressed to her soft hair.

"You're beautiful, Keith—you're wonderful!" She was holding on to him tightly, the words little more than choked whispers, for his ear alone. "I don't care if you're ten times this dirty, this smoky, there's no better place to be right now than in your arms— knowing you're all right!"

He looked over her head at Gram, and held out one arm. Andi thought fleetingly that she should pull back, to give Gram this special time, this special place. But she found herself in a tight triple-hug, with both women crying. "I'm—we're so—so very grateful...."

"We've been praying," Gram told him, "for you—for *all* of you ever since the siren started blowing."

"At first we heard your voice on the scanner." Andi was still clinging to him. "But not—later."

"There wasn't time to talk."

"That's what I said." But then Gram, ever-practical, pushed away. "How about coffee, dear? Or tea?" At the shake of his head, she offered, "A soda maybe?"

"What I'd really like is ice water. Then I'm going home to shower and collapse."

Andi, hurrying to fill a glass and add cubes, mentioned the buckwheat cakes and liverwurst, and he looked almost apologetic. "I appreciate your planning that, but I can't stay awake that long. And this will probably be one of those rare Sundays when I don't make it to worship service."

"That's fine, dear."

Andi suggested, "Perhaps for lunch? Or dinner?"

"Of course!" Gram liked that. "Call when you get up. We can fix pancakes some other time." She asked about the injured firefighters, and he explained that the one kicked by the horse had a broken leg, and the other had face, neck, shoulder and arm burns. He was in a lot of pain, but they hoped he wouldn't need skin grafts or anything.

After Keith left, the women decided they, too, would go back to bed, even for a little while. "Let's sleep as long as possible," Andi suggested. "We don't need more than one of those bananas before going to church.'' Imagine! she thought. Andrea Sarah Barker looking forward to attending religious services!

"That sounds good to me," Gram agreed, covering a yawn with her hand. "Everyone's safe, so I'll sleep soundly."

"Me, too."

Since Keith wouldn't be in the class she'd attended before, Andi considered going into Gram's, but was glad later that she'd chosen Karlyn's. She found that one member was still at the site of the fire, making sure there were no flare-ups, and the irrepressible Jeff had been the one whose leg had been broken while saving the stallion.

She was almost shocked at someone's saying, "We told him that's what he gets for horsing around all the time." But their obvious concern and prayers showed how much they liked him, even though they'd laughed at the remark.

Keith came shortly after their return from church. "That liverwurst kept calling, Gram. Drew me like a magnet."

She hurried to welcome him, but came to a standstill, raised hand curved around his cheek. "You're burned, too."

His grin showed his attempt at reassurance. "Now you won't be able to tell when you make me blush."

Andi tried to respond with a smile, but felt awful. He'd given no indication that she'd caused pain when her cheek pressed against his last night—this morning. He had been so darkened by all that smoke that neither she nor Gram had recognized the redness of his skin!

He obviously didn't want their concern. "I don't think it's going to blister, but trust you'll forgive my not shaving. I'm putting that off as long as possible."

"You look wonderful," Gram assured, placing the heavy griddle on the stove, "just the way you are!"

Keith's wink was a sharing, making Andi feel warm, included. As much for conversation as to share information, she told of looking through the picture album and Bible.

He didn't recall hearing much about his aunt, so, after eating, they went together to look at the letters and genealogical entries. "I agree with Annie—the whole family should know about this," he said. "How about my taking these to work tomorrow and making copies?"

"Would you...make a set for me, too?" Andi requested.

His eyebrows rose slightly, but, though perhaps wondering why she'd want it, he said he would do so. It wasn't long afterwards that he got to his feet, rubbing his lower back with the fingers of both hands and groaning. "I'm gettin' old and rheumatic!"

"I know you, Keith McHenry! You were lifting and pulling and lugging all night, weren't you?" Gram scolded. "What you need is a couple of aspirin and to go back to bed!"

He thrust his shoulders forward, raised them, then pushed them back as far as they'd go before returning them to their usual straight position. "I have to go to Dalton for an hour or so first."

"Must you?"

"I not only must, I *want* to."

Another of your "unbreakable dates"? Andi wondered as he started for the door, then couldn't help but think, And I love that wholehearted grin of yours!

Gram called after him, "You're welcome to come for supper, dear." But it was too late—the screen door had latched shut, and he was gone.

"You go relax, Gram," Andi offered. "I'll clear away things from lunch."

The older woman insisted on helping with that small task, which was taken care of in minutes. Andi indicated she planned to read a while, but Gram said, "I'm going over to the Ramsley's to see how their son is—the one who got burned so bad."

Andi watched her as she went down the steps, crossed the street and headed up the other side. Good! Hurrying to her room, she took the cellular phone from the drawer and punched in the familiar numbers.

"Hello, Andi." Dad sounded genuinely pleased. "I was sitting here with the Sunday paper—and missing you."

"I miss you, too, Dad. More than I expected to."

"Should I feel complimented or insulted?" His chuckle made this a rhetorical question.

"Complimented, Dad. Definitely. I'm appreciating more and more who and what you are."

"The rest of the clan's so horrible that I improve by comparison?"

"Hardly! Keith and Gram and most of the others are so wonderful I'm going to hate leaving."

"When *are* you coming?"

"I'm not sure yet." This is what she needed to talk about, but found difficult. "Perhaps soon."

"So your decisions have been made."

That had not been a question. "Dad?"

"Andi?"

She sensed the smile in his voice. "I feel less and less qualified to try playing God. I don't understand the background of—or how to fix—too many problems...."

"For example?"

Where do I begin? she wondered. "Well, there's Vanessa. Positively gorgeous and with an exceptionally good job—and she's miserably unhappy, though she wouldn't admit to that. Then there's her father, Brad—the one married to a lawyer, remember? Poor self-image, perhaps in part from trying to measure up to her success. Can't or won't keep a job for any length of time.

"At first I thought his receiving a big chunk of money might make things easier. But what he *really* needs is to feel 'wealthier' in the sense of personal accomplishment.

"And there's Gram, one of the finest women I've ever known—"

"You've known her for only a little over a week, dear."

"I realize that, but you should see how *others* love her—and how much she cares for others. She's out right now, Sunday afternoon, checking on the condition of a volunteer firefighter injured in a barn fire last night!

"And she teaches a Sunday School class, and volunteers in the adult literacy project here. And she made all the hamburger barbecue for the carnival this

weekend and helped with the dinner on Friday
night...."

He laughed. "Maybe we can nominate her for a
Nobel prize."

She hesitated, realizing how intense she'd been. "I
guess that did sound like an unimpressive string of
qualities, but I find her to be at peace with herself.
And her neighbors. And with God. Does that make
any sense?"

"Yes, Andi, it does. But you've just been speaking
of two people who probably *shouldn't* receive a windfall."

She nodded, knowing he couldn't see her do so.
"This is confusing to me, too. I hadn't put it in words
before—even in my mind. And, to be honest, my rec-
ommendation as to giving *Gram* money would be
largely because of the pleasure that would give *me*.

"She's already so immeasurably rich—family,
community, friends, church—that she has no need for
what we can give. And though wealth could make it
possible for her to do even more for others, it might
make *them* more expectant, make them feel more
needy, and wanting more from her."

"I understand."

"She and Keith and Karlyn—they're so loving and
loved...." She had to blink away moisture in her eyes
and clear her throat. "They've earned the respect, ad-
miration and genuine regard people have for them.
I'm not sure we have the right to risk that being forgotten."

"How could that be forgotten? You consider
money the root of all evil?"

"Oh, no! Money's just money, and I know it can

be and often is used for good. And I also realize I'm still too much influenced by what happened with Jon.'' She wished Dad would say something. ''I don't want to think that you and I are the only people in the world wise enough to know how to handle it.''

''So where does that leave us, Andi?''

''I—don't know.'' Her voice was choked.

''Do you think staying longer can clarify things?''

''If…there are no further complications.''

''Like?''

''Dad…'' He was usually so busy that she didn't bother him with her problems. Here on the phone, however, it seemed natural to ask, ''You do believe in prayer, don't you?''

''Of course.''

''We never talk about it.''

He sucked in a long, audible breath. ''We haven't talked about many of the things we should have. Will you help me, Andi, to do better in that department?''

''I'll try.'' It was a promise. ''And I could use your prayers right now. You see, I think I've…fallen in love. With Keith.'' That wasn't as hard as I expected, she thought, relieved.

''Like…with Jon?''

His voice sounded neutral, but she suspected he was concerned. ''Not anything like that! Jon was my close friend and, well, we did talk about getting married, and *might* have, had he lived. But—I don't know that I'd ever have been able to completely trust him….''

''Like with all his other women?''

So Dad had known of at least some of them! Was it because of that that he'd hired the investigator? Was that so he could tell her his findings, had she decided to get married?

"I was frustrated at his refusal to withdraw from his perpetual never-never land of playing at being grown-up, with little required but to have fun.... But Keith is a *man*, a truly good man, who cares intensely about the well-being of those around him."

"Of you, also, my daughter?"

"Even me." The wonder of that! she thought. "A stranger who entered his town only eight days ago."

"And—is he 'falling in love' with you?"

"I think so. He likes me, I'm sure of that. But he likes so many people!"

"Have you—" there was a small break "—been— uh...physically close?"

Her little smile was because of his hesitancy about using even these words—and the realization that this was the first time they'd ever had any conversation like this. "Well, when I walked over to his house to see his staircase last evening—"

"His *staircase?*"

No wonder he's confused, she thought. I'm making a mess of what I'm trying to share with him. "He bought this lovely, big, old house and, in trying to restore it, discovered that the woodwork's chestnut, which I didn't realize was special. When I arrived, he was waiting for me and I—walked right into his arms!"

"How deplorable!" He was chuckling! "I'm supposed to be shocked?"

It was impossible to respond lightly. "It's just— how it affected me that I find disturbing. It felt so right. As though I never wanted to leave. As though I belonged there forever.

"I've never had that experience before. And this morning, when he finally came back safely from the fire in which we knew a couple of men had been injured, he hugged me, reassuring *me,* even before drawing Gram in, too.

"Oh, Dad—" it was almost a wail "—I feel *awful.*"

A sigh. "Love is many things, Andi, but its euphoric qualities may have been oversold. Granted, there's nothing more magnificent than the joys and wonder of love. But a lot of pain comes with it, too."

"I know." The loss of Mother. And Jon. And the fear of losing Dad sometime in the future. Gram's grief at Phil's dying—and now concerning Vanessa and Brad. And Gram's father's grief about losing his sister.

"There's something I especially want to tell you, Dad. We were talking about Gram's Aunt Katherine—your mother. There are two of her letters in the family Bible!"

"There are?" Excitement registered in his voice and then, as though cautioning himself not to be too hopeful, he asked, "When were they written?"

"The first was sent to her brother when she ran away from home. The second was about a year later, to your grandparents." There was no easy way to tell him what must follow. "It was left unopened."

"That monster!"

The explosive way in which the word was uttered made her know it wasn't used lightly. "It was found after the death of her parents, between the Old and

New Testaments in the big old family Bible.'' She'd like to give comfort, but the facts must suffice for now. ''Her mother died seven months after Katherine left. Gram thinks she may have starved herself to death.''

''Unless *he* starved her....''

That had crossed her mind, too. ''I suppose that's possible, but is it worth conjecturing about? Especially since her father, also, died within that next year?''

There was an extended silence then, and in a pain-filled voice he said, ''Oh, how Mom grieved for Michael! She so wanted some contact, some communication!''

''He read that letter after they died, and tried to find her. He wrote to her at the Lansing post office box, which was the only clue he had. When that came back, he went there personally, to check, then hired a detective agency—which wasn't successful, either.''

Dad's sigh was almost a moan. ''Mom said she got a job and was in Lansing for over a *year* before coming here.''

''Michael didn't have access to her letter until later.''

''If only she'd known.''

''At least she does now,'' she said, and then shared Gram's account of Michael's death. ''Keith's making copies of the letters and genealogy, so I'll bring them with me when I come.''

''You have no idea how much I appreciate this, dear!''

''But I have a couple of questions, Dad.''

''Go ahead.''

"When I suggested coming—checking on our cousins like this—you seemed only mildly interested in them…perhaps even reluctant. Why didn't you *tell* me about your grandparents? And about your mother? I've always assumed, perhaps stupidly, that they just drifted apart."

"Oh, Andi, it wasn't stupidity on your part. It was deviousness on mine. Only your saintly mother's unstinting love made it possible for Mom and me to live with the knowledge—what we *thought* we knew— that her family hated her, was cruel to her.

"Rightly or wrongly, we decided it was best for you not to be burdened with resentments or hatred concerning them."

"Dad? About your father—you've never been willing to tell me of him. When I've insisted on some answer, all you'd say was that he wanted nothing to do with either of you, and you wanted nothing to do with him."

"That's the big reason Mom didn't pursue trying to get back together. She had no money, so she cleaned houses for people in Michigan—for a time lived in with a family as their housekeeper and nanny…. And then she got to know a friend of her employer's. She'd had no experience with men, never been on a date, so he swept her off her feet. But when he realized she wouldn't give in to his pressures otherwise, he did marry her. She was apparently happy for a time—until she discovered all his other women. And then one of *them* got pregnant, and he left Mom for her.

"It was just about that time that Mom began suspecting she herself was pregnant, with me—but didn't tell John Farrington that. He willingly paid for the divorce, which she got right away as soon as she came to Illinois. So I have *her* name, which she legally changed back to *Barker*."

Chills went up Andi's spine. That poor, dear woman!

"There was no point, she thought, in sending anyone word. She'd *never* be accepted in her 'ultra-religious,' ultra-judgmental home."

"What did she *do?* How did she, and you, survive?"

"I still wonder about that," he admitted. "She took care of children in other people's homes—if she was allowed to take me along. She cleaned other people's houses. We had a garden and sold asparagus and strawberries and cabbage in season.... As soon as I was old enough to use a snow shovel or run errands, I helped out as I could. I've at least told you about that."

"I knew you were poor. And hard working."

He made a small sound—perhaps a short laugh, maybe a grunt. "In the politically correct language of today, we'd have been near the bottom of the 'below poverty level' group."

"No wonder you worked so hard to rise above that!"

"We were determined that I'd get an education, and I did. Miraculously, as it seems now. And my ability to visualize, to see how things might be made or improved, has to be a gift. It doesn't come with just education."

She had never loved and admired him more. "I

want you to know how very proud I've always been of you."

"Thanks, Andi." His words became almost too soft to hear. "And to think I put off telling you this all these years...."

"I understand now."

"My biggest reservations concerning your Pennsylvania project had to do with not wanting you hurt—whether by finding that branch of the family to be as unapproachable and judgmental as our ancestors were, or by being told incorrect things—lies—about Mother."

She was smiling now. "As it's turned out, Dad, they are among the most approachable, *non*judgmental folks I've ever met. So there was even more reason for my coming."

Their conversation continued a few minutes longer, but Andi did not mention her major concern: Was there *any* way she could tell Keith—and Gram—who she was and why she was here?

She climbed into bed and tried unsuccessfully to read—and to sleep. But questions kept coming. How would *she* feel if someone had deceived her so? Could she possibly be objective enough to consider that person's motives? Listen to her rationale?

The alternative was even more painful. Could she, like Katherine, walk away? If she did, would those she'd come to love really care? Would they be hurt—as she would be?

She couldn't leave an address, nor a phone number; even an unlisted one could be traced.

Help me know what to do, God. You know my in-

tentions were good in coming here. I had no expectation of falling in love.

She was still awake when Gram returned and came up to her own room. Just having her in the house helped Andi to finally relax.

Smiling, she slid over on the wooden porch swing as Keith came up the steps two hours later and asked, "Were you able to get a nap?"

"For about an hour. I have trouble sleeping at night."

She thought that he started to say something. "What is it?"

He made a wry face. "I probably shouldn't ask."

"It's okay."

"Is it just since the death of…Jon?"

"Mostly." She continued to meet his gaze.

"Gram mentioned your grieving. I'm—sorry. For you."

"It was very sudden—an accident."

"And you came east, needing time to recover."

"In many different ways."

There was no conversation for a time. Then in a subdued voice, she said, "It's nearly time for me to return."

The hand that had been holding on to the swing's chain became white-knuckled, as from a muscle spasm. Keith's clear-eyed gaze shifted to hers. "Must you leave? So soon?"

"It's been over a week, and I never did go on to New England."

"You're not disturbed by my bringing up the subject of Jon, are you?"

Her hand hovered a moment over his right one before starting to pull back, when she realized how much darker and redder it was than the other. "Keith! Your hand was burned, too!"

"It's not too bad. Not unbearable."

"I wish you'd told me." With sadness she looked back up into his eyes. "I'd have appreciated being included in your hurtings as well as happinesses."

"That sounds like where I'm coming from, too, Annie." His reddened hand reached for hers and lightly squeezed it. With a slight upturn of the right corner of his mouth, he added, "And here goes—complete honesty... I'm going to extricate this hand and replace it with the other—" which he did "—the reason being that yes, it does hurt."

He tried to make light of his injury. "And methinks, my lady, that you've just attempted a change of subject."

She couldn't keep from smiling. "But I am sorry your face and hand—and what else?—are giving you pain."

"Nothing else—at least physically." With a decidedly impish look, he added, "When I was little, my mother's kiss used to heal such things."

She could tease also. "I can call her for you—perhaps she can come take care of that."

"You are delightful, Annie Marker." But his smile gradually disappeared. "I don't want you to go."

"I must. Soon." In spite of her good intentions, she admitted, "It will be with reluctance."

Gram came to the doorway, and Keith said, "I'm inviting Annie to go with me for dinner. I'm starved."

"I'm sure you are. Even with liverwurst, pancakes don't stay with you long."

Andi gave her a little hug on her way in to change clothes. What a sweet, loving woman she was, as well as being understanding and wise.

Wouldn't it be wonderful to have her for a grandmother?

What am I doing? she demanded of herself as she went up the stairs. Am I seriously considering that happening?

"Oh, what a tangled web we weave," she quoted Sir Walter Scott's words softly to herself, "when first we practice to deceive."

Chapter Thirteen

Andi hurried out before Keith came to a full stop in front of Gram's. "Ah, the car instead of the truck."

"Mmm, hmmm. Date night!" His eyes sparkled. "This vehicle has a seat belt in the middle, in case you're open to suggestions."

She laughed, wanting him to believe she thought him joking—which he could be! Fastening the outer restraint, she asked, "And let everyone in Sylvan Falls assume you're interested in that strange woman staying at Gram's?"

"I can think of worse scenarios." The car started down the street. "But right now we must decide where to eat."

She looked sideways at him. "I'm in your hands."

"Wow!" He reached across to rub her shoulder. "You must have more faith in me than I thought."

"I never distrusted you, Keith." *Why must I always respond so seriously when he jokes with me?* she chided herself. *I really must lighten up!*

"Of course not. Although you didn't stay long at my house last night," he added with a wry grin.

Well, she *had* tried to keep from getting too serious—when it was already too late! "It was late. If you hadn't got *some* sleep last night, you'd hardly be functioning right now."

"O-*kay*. You win on that point. And I wouldn't want to be nonfunctioning right now."

She laughed. "Are you on call again tonight—for firefighting?"

"I've told the guys I'll be out of town." He grinned. "So, where are we eating?"

"I'd…prefer some relatively quiet place. Where we can talk."

"That rules out most nearby restaurants. I'm always running into people who want to visit."

"As though *you* don't like that."

"Guilty as charged," he said cheerfully.

"Could we perhaps get take-out Chinese?"

"For two or for three?"

"What?" Why would he ask that?

"Were you thinking of just you and me, or with Gram?"

"I didn't realize *you* were thinking in terms of her."

He reached for her hand, holding it loosely. "Believe me, Annie, my preference *is* for just the two of us. I was afraid you might still feel the need of a chaperon.

"So—" he was beaming at her "—where shall we eat our take-out Chinese for two?"

"Perhaps," she said, feeling uncharacteristically bold in her suggestion, "we could eat at *your* kitchen table—before you show me more of that excellent chestnut woodwork." She had a fleeting moment of wondering if he'd maneuvered her, but couldn't bear to have him think that she didn't trust him.

"What a very good idea, Miss Marker."

He did not park in front of his house when they got back, but drove in by way of the alley. "I don't want folks to know I'm home," he explained, pulling into the garage.

"Uh-oh! Maybe I *should* have held out for a chaperon."

He laughed, that wondrously joyous sound. "During carnival week, especially, I'm sure to get called for *something* if they find me."

She stopped there at the end of the walk. "In that case, let's get back in the car and go somewhere else."

"The key words are, *if they find me*. As of now, we will just go inside. And stay there."

There were still a couple of hours before dark, so she didn't ask about later, when they'd have lights on. They entered by way of a small, cluttered, enclosed porch, where some fireman's equipment was stored, along with boots and work jackets.

The kitchen, painted white with beautiful shades of blue and yellow, appeared to be even larger than Gram's, and more modern. "This is lovely!" she exclaimed. "It would be a dream to cook here—or just relax."

"I'm glad you like it."

Under other circumstances, she'd have considered that trite, but he explained, "The kitchen's the hub of my parents' home, as it's always been of Gram's. It seemed right that this should be my first completed room."

"You did an excellent job and—" she indicated the wainscoting around the lower part of the walls "—I assume this was not chestnut."

"We-e-ll, as embarrassing as it is, I must admit to not at first realizing it was. Which may be just as well—" he shrugged "—since it has at least a dozen coats of paint! I'd probably *still* be working at its removal."

She smiled. "I love these big windows on the south and west sides—being able to look out over your bird feeders and flower beds."

While setting out plates and glasses, he asked, "Which do you prefer? Tea? Coffee? Soda? Milk? Orange juice?"

"They usually serve green tea in Chinese restaurants back home, so I'll choose tea here. Any kind."

"Green tea bags okay?"

"Of course."

The food was seasoned as she liked it, and eating it with this man added immeasurably to her enjoyment and appreciation. She tried to keep him talking, but did have to give some information about her home…without mentioning its twenty-four rooms and that it rested on a quarter-block of prime real estate.

She spoke of college experiences, but going to Michigan State didn't raise as many questions as might have been asked had she said she attended an Ivy League school.

About Dad, she was as evasive as possible. He was a physicist and also had skill with computers, and was with a company in a Chicago suburb. She did feel guilty about that—no actual lies were told, but there was no way the impression she gave was accurate.

He asked again about Jon. "Were you engaged?"

She shook her head. "No date had been set. We'd been friends from way back in elementary school."

His empty plate had been pushed to the side and his forearms rested on the tabletop. "Would you tell me about him, Annie? Gram says you were broken up over his death."

It was late enough that she could no longer have told that his face and hand were darker than normal. He probably couldn't see her too clearly, either, which was just as well. "It was all so—*wrong*. So unnecessary!"

"Meaning?"

"His parents were better off than average, though not really wealthy. They did give him more in the way of material things than—well, than most parents could. But it was his mother's parents who were constantly piling things on their only grandchild."

"What kind of things?"

"Like the new convertible as soon as he got his driver's license. And pilot's school and unlimited funds to have a plane available any time he chose. They did insist on his getting decent marks in prep school—they were determined on his going to Yale. And they paid expenses there."

"What a great deal that was."

She got up and started toward the door. "I hope you don't mind if I turn these on." They squinted at one another until their eyes adjusted to the brightness of the Tiffany-style light over the table. It seemed essential that she see any changes in his expression.

"It *should* have been a 'great deal,' Keith, but on his twenty-first birthday he received an incredible amount of money—no strings attached. And that's how he spent it—with no supervision, no thought for the future! His lifestyle quickly became...well, wild."

"But you continued to see him?"

She drew in a sharp breath and met his gaze.

"I'm sorry, Annie. That was inappropriate. I had no right to ask."

She shook her head. "It's okay. I want you to know what happened. I didn't get along with his new friends. I knew they were freeloaders—just looking for an endless party. But when he was home—when *they* weren't around—we were still together a lot."

Keith remained unmoving, saying nothing, and she went on. "We talked about getting married, had done so for several years—but now I doubt that it would have happened."

She looked up from where she'd been moving the cut-glass saltshaker around and around in small circles. His brown eyes were as warm as she'd remembered, his lips not tight.

Her eyes closed, and when they just as slowly reopened she was focusing on her ringless left hand. "After his death, his family and friends insisted that the diamond necklace he gave me at Christmas meant to him that we were engaged."

There was another long period of quiet, eventually broken by Keith's whisper. "You don't have to go on." His hand covered hers.

"I may never be able to do this again and—you do have the right to know." She did not question why she'd put it that way, why she thought he had that right. "I was with him when he died—that's when my leg was so badly injured. He had been drinking—and going too fast. And I could do nothing for him."

He got up and came around the table to kneel beside her, drawing her close. She was not crying, as she'd done with Gram—not outside, anyway. "He might not have died had he not been given all that money. He didn't have the foggiest idea how to handle it—and I couldn't help him... It destroyed him."

"You don't know that was the reason, Annie. Not everyone needs millions to get in trouble."

And then he was holding her in his arms, his burned cheek hot against hers. "What a lot you've had to bear! Annie, my dear, sweet Annie, I love you."

How many times she'd had someone say he loved her, that he wanted to marry her! Half of Jon's so-called friends had done that—and she'd known it was only for what she was. Her father's daughter. The heiress.

But here, even without his knowing she had any money to speak of, Keith said he loved her.

She drew back enough to look into his eyes—saw the gentleness, the goodness there. She gently cupped his cheek with her hand, longing to tell him how privileged and even blessed she felt by knowing he loved her. The words, "I love you, too," hovered on her lips, but remained unspoken. As she sadly knew they always would. She must at least have the strength to protect him. "You don't know me, Keith. Not at all," she said instead.

"I know what I need to—and so much more."

With one finger he touched her lips as she was about to speak. "I've asked *you* questions—more than I probably had any right to. It's your turn now. What would you like to know about me?"

I must get this back on a lighter level, she thought. "Oh, a little tit for tat, hmm?"

"I've just told you I love you, and it's only right that you're given the opportunity to learn whatever you might want to know about me—*if* you want to know."

One thing had haunted her since their first meeting, but before she asked, she owed him the truth about herself. When she didn't respond right away, he went on. "I hope you can love me, too, but for love to *mean* anything, there has to be honesty. And trust."

Honesty! she thought ashamedly. Trust! In order for love to mean anything! He has so much integrity and thinks I do too... In spite of her good intentions, the words came out. "There is one thing."

"Just one?" Those beautiful dark eyes looking into hers! "I was hoping you'd be interested enough to ask a dozen questions. At least."

Even as guilty as she felt, she couldn't keep from smiling—but only fleetingly. "You said something the day I first came, when you wanted to make sure I wasn't flirting with you...."

"When I *what?*"

"You know—when you couldn't do anything about my car problem because it was late Saturday...."

"That wasn't meant as rejection, Annie. It *was* late."

"I know. But then you looked at the clock and said you must hurry—that you had a date, in Dalton."

His eyes widened, and then it was as though the sun was breaking through—beginning there and increasing until his whole face was filled with his smile. "Oh, Annie!"

As hard as that was, she resisted his arms pulling her back into his longed-for embrace. "Other times, too—even this afternoon—you've had to be in Dalton. Are you...involved with some girl—some woman?"

"Well, there's a *girl* with whom I'm spending a lot of time...."

With the palm of her hand against his chest, she pushed away from him, throat aching. *He doesn't even look apologetic or anything—as though I should be upset!* "It's a good thing we're having our talk tonight." Her voice came out small, tight. *What a fool I've been!* she thought.

"It's not what you think—not at all. But it *is* a commitment, a—"

"It's all right. Of course it is. You had a life before I came, and you'll have it when I'm gone—"

"Hear me out, Annie," he pleaded. "Please."

She turned away. "I just want to go back to Gram's." *I sound like a spoiled, broken-hearted child,* she told herself, *but I feel so stupid. I had no idea I was so vulnerable—that I could be so easily hurt.* "I will leave tomorrow."

Somehow he got around her, was standing with his back against the closed door. "Annie, you're being unfair!"

The emotional turbulence was overwhelming. If

she didn't leave immediately, she'd be sobbing, making an even greater fool of herself. "Let me go."

"Not until you listen—or until you agree to go with me to Dalton to meet Tiffany. Right now—"

"I don't *want* to meet your Tiffany. Or any other female you—" tears were almost unstoppable "—you are like Jon. He—saw nothing wrong with having affairs while saying he loved me!"

He continued standing there, upturned hands stretched only halfway to her. "You're about to reject whatever I say right now. You're willing to throw over everything we have going for us—and that *everything* could be boundless!

"Believe me, I'd prefer explaining in words—if you'd listen. As it is, I'm asking—*begging* you to come with me."

"I…"

"What do you have to lose?"

He doesn't look angry, not even annoyed—just pleading, she noticed.

"Fifteen or twenty minutes to go to the Dalton Hospital. That much again to return. Is that too much to invest in our futures?"

The hospital? Was someone in post-surgery? Or dying? she wondered. She sucked in her breath, knowing she was being unreasonable. Her voice came out choked. "I will listen if you…want me to."

His head tilted to the side; he was considering—what? "I could so easily explain, but would prefer your going."

She sat as close to the passenger door as the seat belt permitted. She'd seldom been more uncomfortable than at this moment, in spite of Keith's talking almost constantly. About a man and his Model-T car. Jeff and his broken leg. His grandfather's recipe for barbecue.... Nothing personal. Nothing requiring a reply.

Only once did she try to get him to turn back, assuring him she'd try to believe whatever he said. He didn't look angry or resentful, just kept driving. And talking.

They parked in the hospital's lot, and he drew her hand through his arm as they crossed the street, keeping it there as they entered the big building. Up in the elevator to the third floor. Greeted by a harried-looking nurse. "Hello, there! You're late today!"

His hand rested for a moment on her shoulder. "I was here early this afternoon, but thought I'd come back—and bring a friend."

"Great!" She gave Andi a quick smile before saying, "She's been crying for hours, and we haven't had time...."

"I know how shorthanded you are, especially on this shift." His patience seemed boundless. "I'll see what I can do."

"Gowns and shoe-covers are on the counter. As usual. Anything you do will be a help."

This was obviously the OB department, but Keith was busy putting on a surgical gown, and Andi couldn't ask who they were visiting. She followed him down a corridor, and he stopped at a wide, plate-glass window, behind which were five babies lined up in minicribs. They all appeared to be full term, two lying there sucking their thumbs, two asleep, and one fussing, though not actually crying.

Near the back of the well-lit room, however, was another small bed. Andi couldn't see a name—nor anything except tiny flailing fists and arms. But the continuous high-pitched crying was loud enough to be heard through the glass. To break the unbearable silence between Keith and herself, she murmured, "That little one's sure unhappy."

He nodded. "Tiffany's having a rough time of it."

Tiffany!

He stood looking through the glass. "We don't get many crack babies, thank God! When we do, I try to help."

"Keith...?" Why can't I keep my mouth shut and just listen? she berated herself. How could I have been so untrusting? So afraid? "Can you ever forgive me?"

He just stood there, biting his lip, otherwise not moving. "Keith?"

His head turned slowly toward her. "What?"

His voice sounded normal, but she wasn't sure. "I—was hoping you could forgive me."

That slow, wonderful smile, his arm coming around her waist to pull her closer.... "I'm sorry I didn't hear you, but I was praying. As to forgiving you, Annie, there's nothing to forgive. I should have just told you."

"Is Tiffany the daughter of—someone you know?"

He shook his head. "But her need's so great! And I've come to love her and the others so very much!"

A short, plump nurse waved, then came to the doorway. "Aren't *you* the unpredictable one?"

"It's Firemen's Carnival Week in Sylvan Falls, Molly."

She included Andi in her smile, but spoke to him. "According to the chart, you've come anywhere from six in the morning, through midday and late afternoon, to now at—" she glanced at the wall clock "—nine thirty-seven. Are you going in now?"

Andi thought that she saw longing in his eyes, so nudged him toward the door. "Go ahead, Keith. I want you to."

That was true, but she was still unprepared for her own emotions as she saw him go in, gowned and masked, and reach down to pick up the screaming infant. Tiffany's little back arched, feet kicking and hands beating the air.

He held her against his shoulder and walked with her. He snuggled her in his arms, and though Andi could neither hear him nor see his lips, she was sure he was talking or singing to the infant. Slowly, ever so gradually, the screams became crying...and finally a hiccuping...before she calmed.

He rocked her in his arms, moving around the nursery, then sitting in the big, comfortable-looking rocking chair that stood in the corner of the room. He held a bottle to the baby's mouth, and Andi watched her eat, her eyes slowly closing, her body relaxed. Finally Tiffany slept.

Coming back down the hallway, Molly stopped beside Andi, a sweet gentleness brightening her plain, middle-aged face. "Anyone who'd give so much of himself for one of these suffering little ones has got to be some special guy! You must be very proud of him."

"Yes. I really am." Andi looked at Keith and the baby—the loving man and the innocent infant so racked with pain. "He's one of the most special people I've ever known."

She stood there, watching. What a father he'd be—and what a husband! she thought. But she knew far too little about either. She dearly loved Dad, but he'd worked night and day while she was growing up, trying to get the business going, then making it grow.

She'd often wished he'd given her more time, but from what she'd just learned she understood much better his all-encompassing drive. He'd *had* to succeed—to prove to himself, more than to others, that Andrew Barker, son of his rejected mother, was not only as-good-as but *better* than competitors!

And poor little Tiffany, agonizing through her first weeks of life! Apparently being held close, being talked and sung to, being *loved*, made even the horrors of withdrawal more bearable.

Andi saw the deepening lines radiating toward Keith's temples. He was smiling at her, and she responded. He got up and, after raising Tiffany so he could kiss her cheek through the mask, gently laid her in her little bed, patting the lightweight blanket around her.

Untying and removing his gown, mask and shoe coverings, he came back out through the little anteroom. Andi met him at the doorway. "Thank you for bringing me."

"I'm glad you came." They were reversing the steps taken perhaps an hour earlier. "A little over a year ago, I saw a newspaper article about these little ones whose mothers had been doing drugs. There was a picture of an elderly woman who, they said, used to come in regularly to rock and love the babies, but she'd suffered a stroke—and they needed volunteers.... I called to ask if they could use the services of a man—and I've done this ever since. Whenever there's a need.''

"Do you usually come more than once a day?"

"I'm committed to once, but at the beginning, when they're first born, I often come before and after work—sometimes instead of eating lunch or before bed—depending on how bad they are, how much agony they're going through.''

"How long have you been working with Tiffany?"

"Ten—no, it's eleven days. But it's not 'working' with her, Annie. I'm just loving her—holding, talking and singing to her, rocking her. Whatever. And when she's well enough, we hope she'll be adopted into some family where she can be loved twenty-four hours a day.''

They were going out the front door when she said, "I admire you very much." He came to a stop, not moving at all, but looking upset. "Is something wrong?"

"Don't admire me for this." He drew in a ragged breath. "I'm doing it because I want to."

She reached for his hand, surprised at its being given reluctantly. "I don't know any other man who would do what you are doing for these tiny, innocent babies.''

As they strolled back to the car, he kept their conversation on the hospital itself and the beauty of the night. Then he unlocked her door first, and walked around to his. "Having trouble with your seat belt?"

She shook her head, feeling unbelievably school-girlish. "Is it all right if I use the middle one on the way home?"

He assured her that it was very much all right.

Chapter Fourteen

They were driving down Main Street when he brought her hand to his lips and kissed the fingertips. "Okay if we go on to my house?"

She said that would be fine. They had not talked much in the car. Apparently Keith was content just being with her, and Andi was trying to decide how much—and *how*—to tell him what he must know.

If there was even the possibility of a future with him, she had to take the chance. Didn't she?

He should be given the opportunity of having input as to what was best. Shouldn't he?

But what if he became angry...rejected her...*hated* her? Could she bear that?

She'd said she was leaving soon, possibly tomorrow. Would he still want her to stay?

Even if he did, she could not remain forever, no matter how much she might like to. Dad needed her. All her life she had been groomed to take over her father's company. Since finishing college, she'd gradually assumed some of the responsibility for more and more departments, which would lead to her eventually taking over when Dad chose to retire—or was forced to.

Keith again parked in the garage and they entered the house through the back porch. It was in the kitchen that he took her in his arms, gently at first, then more tightly, looking down into her eyes. "I love you, Annie Marker—and I want desperately—I *need*—to kiss you."

Even as she clung to him, as her lips moved towards his, she tried to tell herself this was wrong, that his protestation of love was for "Annie Marker," whoever that was.

But that could not keep her from letting him kiss her, from receiving from him this—this… Rational thought ceased as she responded joyously, passionately, with a completeness she had never known, with…

His lips drew away. "Annie, my love…"

Looking up, she *saw* that love, and marveled.

But then her face was against his neck, between his shoulder and cheek, and she was horrified by what she'd done! By what she was doing! *My love,* he had-said! She started to push away.

"Are you all right? You look…ill!"

More ill than you can imagine! she thought with chagrin. "Keith, darling… Please—could we sit down?"

"You are sick. Here, I'll carry you in to the couch."

She shook her head. "No, Keith, I'd prefer here at the table—where we were before."

"If you're sure you won't…" He looked uncertain, but nodded. "Here, sweetheart." Pulling out her chair, he assisting her into it and started to pull his own around, to sit beside her.

She asked, however, that he be across from her, and he hesitated. "Can I get something for you? Some water?"

She hoped the smile she struggled to produce looked more normal than it felt. "Just your full attention. With no interruptions."

His worried eyes were fixed on hers and his hands held hers, thumbs caressing the backs of them. "You've got it—forever, should it take that long."

She looked at those beautiful lips which had a moment before filled her with all-consuming joy—lips she desired more than anything in the world to be kissing right now. And she looked at his strong, capable hands, one of which was fiery red, like his face—the result of his acting out of compassion for others.

"I don't want to do this!" It was an elemental cry—as full of pain as little Tiffany's.

Honoring his promise of silence, Keith simply lifted her hands and leaned over to kiss them.

How can I possibly tell you what I must, when your eyes have looked into mine so trustingly? she asked silently. Yet I can't put it off any longer. She finally managed to speak. "Almost everything you know about me is a lie, Keith. It was not because of car trouble that I came to Sylvan Falls, that I came to your dad's garage, that I'm staying at Gram's bed-and-breakfast. I bought this older used car expressly for the purpose of—"

"May I say one thing?" he whispered.

She'd never get this told if he interrupted. "Just one. After that, I'm holding you to your promise."

"Agreed." He shifted on his chair, hands still holding hers. "I don't *care* that you drive a used car, Annie. Or whatever it is that's troubling you so much! It's *you* I love. We can work together to overcome other difficulties. I'm not minimizing that it will take a while to fix up this place." He glanced around. "Or we can sell it and buy another you like better. We won't live in luxury, like you could have with Jon, but we'll be together. And *loving*."

This is even harder than I anticipated! Andi thought. You're reassuring me because you think I'm poor... "I stopped outside of town and *caused* that car trouble," she continued, "as our chief mechanic instructed me. And yes, I did say the *chief* one—he's over a whole department in the business created by my father and owned by him. And me. The place in which I told you I worked in Accounting before coming here."

His thumbs stopped moving against her skin and his eyes widened. She continued. "Prior to that, I spent time in Promotion and Advertising, and when I return I'll rotate through Research and Development, which means I'll have been through all departments."

She drew in a big breath—needing to before going on. "In other words, I must go back, because I'm being prepared to someday replace my father as head of our...enterprise."

Horizontal lines formed across his forehead, and his lips pressed tightly together, showing the effort it took to keep words from spilling out. She started again. "I came here deliberately, to meet Gram and the rest of you."

His hands released hers and lay palms-down on the edge of the table as he leaned back in his chair. His dark brows drew together as his expression grew solemn, stony.

She looked at her own hands, still where he'd left them. "My reason for doing this—the *necessity* for doing this—was fulfilled today." Her gaze moved upward and saw the hurt on his face. Leaning forward, she burst out, "That's not because of your profession of love or sharing about Tiffany. I had no idea, no expectation of that. It was my learning more about Katherine. And that your grandfather, Michael, did love her, did try to find her—"

"Katherine?" The name exploded from him.

"You promised, Keith," she reminded, knowing he'd not meant to speak. "I do understand how difficult this is to follow. And to believe."

His nod was firm, his expression grim. She explained, "Keith, my father, Andrew Barker, is the son of Katherine."

Shock—that was the only way to describe his sitting there, lips parted, face frozen, eyes staring into hers. "My grandmother grieved her whole life over the separation between herself and her family—from Michael.

"She died, never knowing how much he cared."

He was straining forward, leaning across the table, motioning with his hand toward his lips.

Her sigh, her saying, "I know this is difficult," must have shown that she understood his need to speak.

"Then why didn't she write *again?*"

"How I wish she had! She stayed in Michigan a full year, hoping. She would have remained longer, but she got married. And remember—from what Gram said, even at 18 she'd never dated and knew nothing about men. She'd apparently believed everything he said, but then he got another woman pregnant so he divorced Katherine, and married her—sort of like what happened to your sister, Karlyn."

Andi assumed he understood that, for he nodded. "Grandma had too much pride to tell him when she found that she, too, was pregnant. And knowing how rigid her parents were, she came to terms with what she considered fact. If they were unwilling to have anything to do with her as a runaway, they'd never accept her as a soon-to-be-divorced woman awaiting the birth of her child."

"But..." His hand reached toward hers, though he caught himself before saying or doing more. Pushing himself back in the chair, he sat ramrod-straight, self-control starkly evident.

She explained what little she knew of the poverty, struggles and difficulties of Katherine and Andrew, and then of his doing exceptionally well within the very first company where he worked and of his marrying her mother.

"Mother gave unequivocal support to his starting his own business, and it was the income she earned teaching that made it even possible. Those early financial struggles, of which I've spoken—thus giving you the idea that I came from a poor family—were very real during my childhood."

She cleared her throat. "My friendship with Jon

began back in third grade, when he beat up a bully who made me cry by poking fun at my rummage-sale clothing. I was...insecure. And it felt so good to have someone besides my parents and Grandma Katherine care about me. Incidentally, she was a dear, wonderful woman, but she died when I was young, before I thought of asking about her past." If only I had, Andi thought, though she wouldn't have burdened a child with such pain.

"Until Jon's death, my hunger to learn more about the Pennsylvania Cousins—which is how I always thought of you—was a back-of-the-mind, someday-I'll-do-it sort of thing. But then it struck me that Jon was the last of his line—as *I* am the end of Katherine's. It became more and more important that I learn about her brother's family. Were they more like *her* or like her parents? Yet I feared it would be impossible to find out if I came as Andrea Barker, daughter of 'Andrew Barker, the Electronics Wizard.' So many newspaper and magazine articles have been written about him. I was sure someone here would recognize his name."

The flickering of his eyelids and tightening of his jawline showed his familiarity with that name and sobriquet. "So I arrived as 'Annie Marker'—and have come to love all of you, to respect you, and to be *proud* of being part of your family."

She had to brace herself for the most difficult part! "But the other kind of love—the man-woman kind—has entered the picture. Believe me, dear, I did not try to make you love me—never thought of such a thing. I was just grateful you were so warm and open with me—that you treated me as a friend."

His upturned hands extended toward her, face entreating—and she nodded permission for him to speak. "Couldn't you have told us before this? Given us the chance to know 'Andrea Barker,' as you were learning about us?"

"Do you truly believe any of you could have been as free and open with *Andi*—" she deliberately emphasized the name to indicate how she thought of herself "—daughter of the extremely wealthy, well-known Drew Barker—as you were with 'Annie'?"

He rose from his chair and paced the room. His still-tense fingers combed back through his hair, and his voice was tight. "But I feel...*violated*, almost...."

"Never in my wildest dreams did I consider the possibility of falling in love while here." Could he sense how filled with wonder she was—how awed by this? And how sad it was to have to apologize when speaking of it?

"This has changed everything. Because of future responsibilities, I *can't* stay. And you have such strong family and community ties. And your job, and this house—" she looked around "—that I can't ask you to leave."

The silence seemed to last forever. She had no idea what more to say. Actually, there was much she *could* say, but... She finally whispered, "I love you very much, Keith. But please, don't feel you must say or do anything tonight. Just, if you *can*, try not to hate me."

Blinking back the moisture in her eyes, she slid back her chair, pushed herself to her feet, and started for the front hallway. Keith got there before her, and she saw him through her tears—big, strong, and holding out his arms. For only a moment she resisted, then was clinging to him, being enfolded, being held tight to the magnificent strength and security of this man she loved.

Her face was buried against his neck. "I'm sorry—"

"Shhhh." A whisper. Comforting. Reassuring. "It's all right, sweetheart. I understand, at least in part, why you felt you had to do it this way."

She thought of Tiffany, the tiny baby in agony because of the habits of her mother, being held and comforted by him. Here Andi, the heiress, was also in such great pain because of the sins of her forebears!

Her eyes remained closed as she moved her head, her lips searching for his, her elemental need of connectedness and hope and love overriding whatever good judgment she'd thought she possessed.

Joy. Security.

The kiss was over, as it had to be sometime. But she did not want to leave his arms. She could hardly bear to think of leaving his life, but she said, "I have to go."

"Not yet. Please."

"I must." The palms of both hands pushed gently against his chest. "And I'll leave Gram's in the morning."

His arms tightened. "We can work this out. We will!"

She wanted to believe that. "How?"

"I—don't know yet." She struggled to free herself, but he didn't release her. "What you said was... difficult to assimilate. I had no suspicion of any of this, Annie. Or *Andi*, I guess it is from now on."

He was trying to reassure, but she fretted, "When you tell Gram and the others——?"

"At the moment," he said slowly, "perhaps it's best not to discuss it with anyone...."

You don't want anybody to know what I have done, she thought. And that you love me. She bit her lower lip to still its trembling, but he went on, "...Unless, possibly, with your father."

They were attempting to feel their way through the quagmire of past and present. At first his suggestion seemed illogical, then began to make sense. "Perhaps that could help. He knows about you—that I love you. And I *would* like you to meet, even by phone."

He walked with her through the end of the dining room and under the large archway on the right to the cozy fireplace room with mellow wood paneling and floor-to-ceiling shelves jammed with books, magazines and papers.

A comfortable-looking couch covered with what looked like technical papers and periodicals was to the right of the doorway into the front room, where she'd been before. Stands and chairs were casually placed, and an open book lay face down on a recliner.

He handed her the phone from the old rolltop desk, and it was only moments before she heard Dad's voice. "Hello, Andi. How are things in Sylvan Falls?"

"Quite good, Dad, in spite of the rain and—other things I'll tell you about later." She was holding the phone so Keith could hear also. "Keith and I want to talk with you. Here he is now."

"Hello, Mr. Barker."

"Ah, so it's Mr. *Barker.*" Dad sounded amused. "Things have changed."

"Yes, sir. Quite appreciably." Keith had accepted not only the phone, but her hand. "You see, your daughter and I have fallen in love."

"And that complicates things, doesn't it?"

Andi's head was against Keith's so she could more easily be in on this three-way conversation. "You expected this call?"

There was an infinitesimal pause. "Will you be disappointed if I admit to that?"

Andi laughed, then explained to Keith, "If I'm not mistaken, my father has had somebody here, checking on me."

"It's worse than that, Keith," he admitted cheerfully. "I was checking on many things, including you. The important part is that you passed with flying colors—getting my daughter to help barbecue chicken, inviting her to a family picnic, taking her on the merry-go-round...."

"I'm not sure, Mr. Barker, that I regard this as humorously as you do." Keith did, indeed, look less than happy. "How would *you* feel if you found you'd been under surveillance—especially when you were dating a most remarkably wonderful woman?"

The response was immediate. "I'd hate it, Keith. And be tempted to hate the guy who did it to me. However, if you were me, the overly wealthy father of that most wonderful woman who went off on a half-cocked investigation of her own—tell me, would you have done differently?"

Keith's face screwed up. Then, rumpling Andi's hair with his hand, he admitted, "That does put a different spin on things. I might—have done the same.''

"Andi," Dad asked, "how many are presently aware of our situation?''

"Only Keith. And that's because he told me he loved me…After that, I *had* to tell him you are Katherine's son, and that you're the founder and owner of our company.'' She hesitated before adding, "It became necessary to say why I can't stay—why I must return to Chicago. To help you.''

"And to eventually take over.'' Dad's voice sounded tired, almost sad. "It's a fearsome burden, Keith. Sometimes I almost wish it need not be thrust upon her.''

She responded into the phone, but her words, her gaze, were for Keith. "That didn't seem a burden before. As you know, I've enjoyed the work and the challenge. But when—*if* we marry, I'd want more time with my husband than you were able to give Mother and me.'' That sounded harsh, but she couldn't change the truth.

"We need to talk more about that time in our lives. But right now, we're faced with more urgent matters.'' Then Dad was asking, "So, Keith, what do you suggest be done now?''

"Well, first things first. May I have permission to ask your daughter to be my wife?''

"Sure, Keith, you may ask. And the two of you would have my blessings.''

Andi broke in. "I have a suggestion worthy of consideration, Dad. How about coming east and meeting your family—all of them?''

"Excellent idea—if my assumption's correct that I

arrive as myself. But I have a couple of concerns. First, do you need time to get them over the shock? And, secondly, are they going to hate you—and me?"

Keith responded to that. "Annie—*Andi* will have to explain to them, as she did to me, her need to be incognito while finding out more about the family."

"Are you—both of you—willing to run this by MaryJean?" Andi heard the whispered rustle of paper indicating that he was checking that ever-present appointment book. "Should it meet with her approval, I could fly in and be there by early evening tomorrow."

"I can pick you up at the airport."

"That's not necessary, Keith, but thanks. If you'll give directions, I'll rent a car and drive there."

She turned the phone over to Keith after saying, "I'll call you, Dad, after talking with Gram...."

Chapter Fifteen

Rain. Pouring-down-in-sheets rain, dripping-from-tree-and-roofs rain, splashing as vehicles went by. To Andi, however, this day was beautiful, the world was wonderful, and she found herself humming as she got dressed.

She was head-over-heels in love, for the very first time in her life—and Keith loved *her*.

She hurriedly got dressed, and ran downstairs to talk with Gram, who had gone to bed before she had returned from Keith's last night. At her place at the kitchen table was a sheet of white paper.

Dear Annie,
I hope you're not reading this till midmorning, but whenever it is, you'll find a big dish of strawberries ready for you in the refrigerator. I'm sure you can find enough other food around to keep from starving.

I have several errands to run, but, since your car's now fixed, you won't be housebound.

I should be back by noon or soon after.

Andi held it in her hands, smiling at Gram's having scratched out *MaryJean,* and replaced it with *Love, Gram.*

My first note from anyone in this family! she thought happily. May there be many more!

She wondered if Keith had been able to sleep. Might he have already gone to work? She ate toast with peanut butter and was enjoying the berries when she heard his quick step on the front porch. "Good morning," she greeted, hurrying to meet him in the hallway.

Lifting her with no more apparent strain than he'd have with little Traci, he soundly kissed her before setting her back on her feet. "You're right, Andi, it is a good morning—at least this part."

"Did you sleep?"

"With a smile on my face!"

She laughed, thinking the same applied to her. "Gram left a note saying she's doing errands."

"She's always on the go," he marveled. "I'm running just a little late, but you mentioned that you'd like to see where I work."

She followed Keith in her own car to the mammoth brick building in Dalton, and when he used his electronic card to open doors and elevators, she noted that the surveillance system was similar to that in Chicago's Barker Building. As they walked through the labyrinthine passageways, she pointed out equipment in various offices that had come from her family business.

She was introduced as "my friend, Andi," without mention of a last name, and she understood his uncertainty as to which one to use. Then they were in his light, airy, office. It looked neatly organized, without a book or paper out of place, which surprised her a little, considering his back porch and fireplace room.

"I'm impressed," she said, looking around. "You didn't tell me you rate a corner office!"

He laughed. "There happen to be three of them here—and I was delighted to be moved directly into this one when the building was renovated two years ago."

"Would you have time to show me some of what you do?"

"In a moment." Taking an oversize folder from a filing cabinet, he started for the open doorway. "Right now I must deliver this to Ben. He was gone by the time I finished it on Friday."

She sat in his chair at the computer until he returned, assimilating at least some of the importance of his responsibilities. There seemed a good feeling among the employees, too—though she knew that superficial first impressions proved little.

She was amused by those who stopped by, saying they were looking for Keith. She had no doubt that they were checking her out, wanting a closer view of this "friend." After their tour, he walked her back to her car. Knowing they were being observed, Keith kissed her briefly on the cheek before they parted.

Gram had returned by the time Andi got home, and they sat at the kitchen table with tea and bagels.

"Keith and I called my father last night," Andi told her, "and this morning I followed him up to see his office."

Gram's eyes seemed even brighter than usual. "I hope everything's going well."

For Dad or for us? "It seems to be. Dad will be in this area late tomorrow afternoon. I hope...it's okay if he stops to visit."

"Of course, Annie! I'd very much like to meet him. And he's welcome to stay overnight, or as long as he can. As my guest, of course."

She'd heard of small-town hospitality, but Andi was convinced this was more than that. She blinked back tears of happiness at the prospect of the cousins meeting. "I'm sure he'd like to do that."

She had to preface what she was about to say. "I want you to know how much I've come to love and appreciate you and your family during this time I've been with you."

"You're—leaving, aren't you?"

Sadness, almost dismay, filled those dear, expressive features and voice. "I do have to go soon. I'm needed back home. But first, I must tell you some things about myself."

Gram's head moved from left to right. "That's not necessary, Annie."

"I appreciate that, but it *is* necessary because...it involves all of us." She drew in a deep breath. "And what I'm about to say is *especially* difficult because you once said you believed I have integrity—and I know how highly you regard that."

She kept her eyes on Gram's, seeing uncertainty

begin there. "I have not been honest with you, but I hope you'll give me the opportunity to explain."

There was a slight hesitation. "I'll—try, Annie."

"First of all, I was not on my way to New England when I came here. I deliberately drove from Illinois to meet you and your family...."

Her explanation to Gram was longer and even more difficult than the one she'd given Keith. A number of things bothered Gram, but one the older woman kept coming back to. "My father *would* have believed Katherine. He'd have tried to help!" With tears in her eyes, she cried, "He loved her."

"That's what I had to find out. We couldn't imagine the life she'd lived at home, raised by unbendable rules, rather than love." Andi paused, thoughtful. "Had I been in that situation, I might very well have had her insecurity—her dread of more rejection—"

"And your car trouble?" Gram asked, confused.

"I created that by loosening a belt just outside of town, causing that noise. I wanted to arrive at the garage too late for Zack or anyone to work on it that Saturday, hoping to be directed to your bed-and-breakfast. Wanting desperately to get to know you."

Gram sank back against the chair. "But—*why?*"

No wonder she's perplexed! Andi thought. I'm doing an awful job of explaining. She has every right to be upset or angry, but looks mostly puzzled. "I hope my reasons make you happy, Gram, not upset. You see—" dear God, help me not to mess this up—help her understand "—my dad is Andrew Barker, the only son of Katherine, your aunt. He is your first cousin."

Confusion, surprise, disbelief and joy vied for supremacy on Gram's face, and Andi hurried on. "Grandma Katherine adored Michael, your father. And she did try to make contact with him and their parents, but getting no response, she was convinced they wanted nothing to do with her."

"Why didn't she try again?"

Andi answered that and many more questions. "I am so very pleased to learn what Michael was like— and so is my dad." She drew in a deep breath. "I felt that I should come incognito, as Annie Marker instead of Andi Barker, a name you just might have recognized....

"Grandma Katherine died when I was still a child, during that period when Dad was struggling to get his business on a secure footing. So what I've shared about how poor we were was true then." Perhaps it wasn't necessary to say that, but she wanted to emphasize that not everything was a lie.

"Dad worked his way through college, and became a physicist—with an incredible gift for electronics, and for visualizing and management. Starting with next to nothing, he succeeded in establishing an electronics empire known around the world."

Gram sat shaking her head. "I'm seldom speechless, as you've undoubtedly noticed, but *this* just about did it!"

"I know it's a shock, and I'm sorry. But I—wanted so badly to get to know all of you."

Gram reached for her knife and started spreading cream cheese on her bagel, then replaced both of these on her plate. "I thought when you kept asking to see all those pictures and talking about my ancestors that maybe you were just being nice to an old lady. I had no idea—"

Andi again covered the hand resting on the table. "I needed the information. But came to love *you,* Gram."

Unexpectedly, Gram started to blot her eyes, and it was all Andi could do to keep from crying along with her. But then the older woman was smiling through her tears. "But isn't it *wonderful* how God worked things out? I came to love you as a wanderer in need of healing. What I found was a beloved relative—the one who could bring our broken family together again!"

Gram asked what time the plane was scheduled to arrive at the airport and Andi explained, "It's a company plane, so the determining factor will be when he gets away from the office."

"Oh." Gram cocked her head, surprised. And she asked many questions as they spent much of that and the next day with the vacuum cleaner, mop, window cleaner and garden tools.

It made no difference when Andi tried to reassure Gram that Dad would be so intent on getting to know *her* that he wouldn't even notice their having worked this hard. She was also unable to talk Gram out of baking pies.

"You almost made it by 5:30, Dad!" she cried, hurrying down the walk to throw her arms around him.

He was dressed casually in slacks, cotton-knit shirt and loafers, and greeted her with a bear hug. "You look great, Andi.'' One arm remained around her as he reached to shake Keith's hand. ''And I'm very pleased to meet you.''

''And I, you, sir.''

''Enough of the 'sir' bit, if you don't mind.'' But Drew's eyebrow raised as he added, ''Though I understand it's intimidating to meet me like this.''

Gram came out of the front door and started down the steps. ''Andrew?''

He reached out both hands for hers. ''MaryJean! My daughter's told me so much about you that I'd have known you anywhere. I'm grateful to finally be meeting.''

''This family reunion's been far too long in coming, and what's really sad is that it had to wait till we're this old.'' She smiled then. ''But at least you're here now.''

They visited in the kitchen as final touches were made to the meal, which they enjoyed around the table. Andi and Keith said little, attention riveted as Gram and Dad tried to pack into this first get-together many of the happenings of generations.

''I like your father,'' Keith said when, meal completed, the older two went into the TV room. He and Andi put things away and washed dishes.

''And he likes you.''

''I was afraid he'd be—more formidable.''

''Oh, he can be, in business—when occasion demands. But he's warm and real, where I'm concerned.''

''There's no doubt about how important you are in his life, Andi. I'm almost surprised he's not trying harder to keep you from getting involved with someone here.''

"You may have caught a veiled reminder or two?"

"Yes, but—"

"He does approve of you, which," she said dryly, "is a first. It would have been hard not to like Jon— but there was no way Dad wanted me married to a playboy like him! He considered several others as possibilities, but I did not.... And then I met you."

Gram and Dad were sitting on the couch, the large album on their knees. Keith and Andi drew up chairs to listen to the piecing-together of family lore and memories.

It was late when Keith left, with Andi walking him to the porch. "Did you see Tiffany today?" she asked.

"Just once—and she seems much better. At least she can finally relax now, and sleep. I'm going to miss her when she goes to her adoptive family, whenever that is."

She asked Keith to sit on the swing with her. "I promise not to keep you long, but...there are some things...." His arm was around her shoulders. "This may sound premature but...you would like to have children, wouldn't you?"

"Your children—of course." He frowned, probably realizing why she asked. "However, if your business pressures and such indicate you *shouldn't*..."

"I have to admit, I'd never thought much about it until coming here—which seems almost scary now." During the ensuing silence, she almost wished it hadn't been necessary to mention that.

"You're so loving with my nieces and nephews. And so concerned for Tiffany."

"It was the way you held that tiny baby—the way you cared for her. If I'd ever doubted it before, I knew then I had to face the fact that I truly love you. Oh, Keith, I do want you to be the father of any children I might ever have. My husband in every sense of the word. For ever and ever!"

"Amen!"

An affirmation. A prayer. A commitment.

Drew had planned to leave the following morning, but was convinced to stay an extra day. Glancing around to make sure no one was around to overhear him, he walked with Andi through Sylvan Falls's small park, toward the ball field. "I have no doubts about your love for Keith, or his for you, dear. And I concur—he is a fine young man; he'd do everything in his power to be a good husband. I'd gladly have him as my son-in-law, Andi. But I must know if you'll decide to stay here after you're married."

She stopped. "We both realize that's impossible."

"Can he be content away from here? There was a tremendous sense of belonging and pride when he showed me his house and his town. And the firehouse named for his grandfather."

His look was piercing. "And I gather he still has no conception of our holdings. Our house. Our grounds. The responsibilities you have."

Did he notice my fidgeting with the button on my blouse? she wondered. She brought the offending hand down to her side. "This has all happened so quickly...." I'm trying to excuse my negligence, she confessed silently. Of course I should have told him.

He went on as though she hadn't spoken, "What about his present position? He's obviously highly thought of, and must make a good salary. He's earned that corner office—it wasn't a gift. And there was no doubt when he took me there today that he loves his work, and is liked and respected."

"I sense a *however* coming...."

"*However*—" his little smile seemed to hold a hint of sadness "—you must face the reality of its being difficult for him to leave. Is what you have to offer— everything marriage to you offers—enough to make up for what he'd be giving up?" He added, "What happens if he goes with you, then finds that—should he choose to return—being away has made it impossible to go back to the way things were?"

She'd winced as she stepped on a small rolling stone, and her leg hurt, but it wasn't the physical aspects of this walk that most bothered her. The thought of Keith's leaving was unbearable. "I've fretted about that, Dad. And more."

"Would you permit me to offer him a vice-presidency?"

"You *can't*, not right off, anyway. For your sake and his. And the company's. I think he's exceptional in everything he does, but we don't know if he can, or would *want* to, handle such different responsibilities."

They sat side by side on the bottom bench of the small grandstand that overlooked the baseball field and the empty factory buildings beyond. "What I'd like, Dad, is for Keith—and Gram, too, if she would—to go home with us. It's not just my wanting them to see how well Katherine's kid has done—'' her arm slid around him and her cheek rested against his shoulder "—but it's essential that they see how things *are*. That they realize I am needed there.''

His head tilted to rest against the top of hers. "My thoughts exactly.''

Andi had tried to prepare them during the week before they came, but Gram was "downright flabbergasted'' by the house and grounds. Keith stood there in the drive, which circled around the marble fountain with its four graceful angels, and exclaimed, "And I said to you that it might take a while to fix up my place!''

She realized how overwhelmed he was feeling. "I like your house, Keith. I truly do.''

Andi and Dad had left work midmorning to meet them at the airport and bring them here. Now his arm was around Gram's shoulders as they walked up the three stone steps, opened the massive wooden door with its lion-head knocker, and went inside.

"This is fabulous, Drew.'' Gram's eyes were huge. "I had no idea....''

"Jan and I bought it at auction several years before her cancer was diagnosed. Our business wasn't as big or well-known then, and we thought entertaining here...'' He started over. "Even as her illness progressed, she oversaw the many repairs, the decorating and landscaping. I'm proud of her and the great job she did.''

They entered the huge parlor which, like Gram's, was to the right, off the formal entrance hall. Andi appreciated Carol's having turned on the lights directed toward the life-size, gold-framed painting centered on the far wall.

"Your wife, Drew?" Gram walked toward it. "Jan?"

He nodded. "Done after her death by a portrait artist in Boston. From a candid shot I took of her right after we'd moved in here." He cleared his throat. "It's exactly like her—that eager, welcoming smile, her hand reaching out to everyone."

"She is so beautiful, Drew." Her voice was hushed.

"She was, in every way—not just physically. Kind, loving, caring. Gentle, yet strong." His voice was soft with remembering. "I wish you could have known her."

"Perhaps, in a way, I do. Your daughter has inherited many of those qualities."

His smile came slowly, directed first toward her, then Andi. "You're right. I have been doubly blessed."

Later, as they were eating the delicious meal prepared and served by Carol, he described some of the difficulties gone through in restoring their home. Not only were there the anticipated problems with plumbing, electricity and heating, but also with things like finding someone with enough expertise to repair plaster moldings around chandeliers and upper walls.

He smiled acknowledgment when she marveled at things turning out so perfectly. "But this house has been needing something more—and we welcome you two as the first of my relatives to enter our home."

House. Home. Andi had not suspected such feelings.

He whisked their guests off to the plant, where they remained for hours. Andi deliberately stayed home. He'd be conducting them throughout the complex, introducing Keith as an engineer from Pennsylvania. It seemed best for now that he not be associated with her.

She sorted through accumulated mail and had taken care of the most urgent items before stopping midsentence when she heard the car. Hurrying downstairs, she took Gram to look at flower beds and plantings, while Dad and Keith closeted themselves in the den. They had to be called for dinner, where the conversation turned to carpenters and landscape gardeners, before shifting to Sylvan Falls.

…Karlyn and her children were going to a church family camp the following week, "…even though the kids are a bit young, don't you think?" said Gram.

…The wife of one of Zack's mechanics had been in an automobile accident, but was coming along fairly well.

…The man Gram was tutoring had asked her to help him teach another driver to read….

It was only after Carol removed their dessert dishes and refilled their cups that Andi asked about their tour. "That plant—that business is mind-boggling!" Gram stated. "All those departments and all those people. There must be almost as many working there as in all of Sylvan Falls!"

Dad nodded, obviously refraining from saying that was an underestimate.

"It went far beyond my expectations, too," Keith

admitted. "I was especially impressed by Research and Development. That staff and equipment are unbelievable—and you have so many projects going on at the same time!"

"Did any of it make sense?"

He laughed shortly. "Not much, but, knowing the degree of confidentiality necessary there, I wasn't about to ask."

Dad's lips twitched. "Had you done so, they'd have known you didn't appreciate the sensitivity of what they're doing. Their answers would have been gobbledygook."

Andi explained, "Now you can better understand my rotating through all departments. I'm now in Research and Development. After that, I'll begin serving as Dad's assistant."

"Frankly, I'm tired," Drew stated. "I've done nothing except work all my life, and I want to be able to just get away occasionally. To enjoy life, travel, play golf, just plain relax. It's true that I have excellent people heading departments, and Sam Jordan, a man who has been with the company from the beginning, has filled in for me sometimes, and has done an excellent job." He glanced at Andi, who nodded. "But as time goes on, I want to gradually turn over more and more responsibilities to Andi."

"I'm confused," Keith admitted. "This is privately owned, right? Not controlled by stockholders?"

"Correct. But there's no way I can stay on top of everything, so all department heads get together on a regular basis."

Keith had been sitting beside Andi, holding her hand, but now let go of it and looked at her with—

awe? "I'm just beginning to understand why you have to be here. And why you're concerned about time for family. For me."

Her heart sank, but she said, "If only I'd settled down earlier—!"

"But in that case, dear," Gram murmured, "you might never have taken time to come find us."

Dad nodded. "I never thought much of what-ifs as a way of life. And anyway, it was my fault—the load increased gradually, and I was so used to carrying it that it took too long for me to accept what should be obvious to anyone—I am expendable."

"We *both* had to think more seriously about other things, and for some we need input from both of you."

So they told in detail about the second part of Andi's purpose in going to Pennsylvania: to find out not only what the relatives were like as people, but how they handled money. "Dad and I are in the process of changing our wills, and we were trying to decide where, and to whom, some of our money should go. We discussed sharing some with relatives, but Mother's only cousin has—well, she's been less than law-abiding, to put it mildly! And because an infusion of money had proved so disastrous in Jon's case, and for others we know, I was very concerned.

"So, partly because I've often wished to know you, I came up with the proposal of going to Sylvan Falls and finding out if our Pennsylvania Cousins would probably be more helped or hurt by receiving some of it."

She wished someone would say something. Gram, head cocked and forehead wrinkled, looked as though she wasn't sure she was hearing correctly. And Andi only wished she could read what was in Keith's mind.

"It turned out that I had a *lot* to learn about humility. As I confessed to Dad, the longer I was there, the more I felt like an idiot child trying to judge and control people. I am convinced that getting a great deal of money wouldn't hurt either of you. In fact—" she looked toward Dad "—I'd like to give them at least as much as we discussed—"

"Now wait a minute!" Keith pushed back his chair and was on his feet. "That is *not* why we're here."

"Please sit down, Keith." Dad's voice was quietly firm. "You asked if our company is privately owned—and it is. This property is also, of course. Plus...other things.

"So what's to become of all of it—" Drew made an outward sweeping gesture, "once I'm gone? Andi is emphatic about not wanting it all for herself, so we've been trying to decide how to go about sharing some of it."

Keith's face was a study as he looked at her. "Like in Sunday School, where you listed universities and social services and research for cures...." With a look of disbelief, he sank back into his chair. "And family...."

"And family," she repeated.

Dad looked from one to the other. "So she went there and stayed at your place, MaryJean—and found so much more than anticipated."

No decisions were made that evening. Andi, not knowing how to interpret the change in their attitude toward her—their apparent withdrawal—slept almost as poorly as she used to before making that trip east.

Chapter Sixteen

Early morning came, and she lay there, wide awake, until nearly five. The sun wasn't up, but the brightness in the east and increased lightness indicated it soon would be.

She had difficulty deciding what to wear—how to get ready for her day. Indecision, she thought. That's not among my usual faults. But how can I bear it if Keith decides he can't handle this—that he doesn't want to marry me?

There was no way she could settle for less than total commitment, less than a marriage before both God and man! And if she married Keith, that would be incomplete if they didn't have at least one baby, created by their sanctified love—a child he would hold with even more love and tenderness than that with which he'd cradled Tiffany.

She got dressed and went to the computer. But even the knotty business problem she'd been working on didn't hold her interest now. She went down the stairs and out the French door leading from the dining room onto the patio. A young artist friend of Mother's had designed and laid these mosaic tiles in an exquisite pastoral scene of handsome shepherd and beautiful shepherdess on a grassy hillside with their sheep.

This had been one of her favorite spots, and on this beautiful morning she slipped out of her sandals and walked barefoot across the dew-sparkled, manicured lawn to the rose arbor. Her fingertips trailed across the white-painted seat, verifying that most of the dew had precipitated onto overhead vines, leaves and brilliant red buds and flowers.

Breathing in the sweet fragrance brought back the memory of this being her refuge when Mother was dying. She did not come for a long time afterwards. Nor following Jon's death.

Why now, she asked herself, am I here? Leaning her head back against the wooden latticework, she looked up through the old vines, their thick, green leaves almost blocking out the blue of the cloudless sky.

Her eyes closed—then opened abruptly as she pulled back as far as possible into her sanctuary. Footsteps were coming this way, and the slanting rays of the sun made a long, skinny shadow on the grass. A voice—Keith's voice—was asking, "May I join you, Andi?"

Her hand reached toward him, and he accepted it, looking very serious as he sat beside her. "We must talk."

No greeting as such. No kiss—not even a smile.

"I'm sorry, Andi."

Oh, no, God! Please... "What is it, Keith?" Her

voice was quiet, hopefully not betraying how alone she felt.

"I want you to know how much I appreciate what you were trying to do." He shifted, turning more directly toward her. "It must have been very difficult for you to come to Sylvan Falls. To us—"

"No, Keith, it wasn't," she interrupted. "I enjoyed—all of you. And your town. And learning about my grandmother."

"—We should have discussed more things while we were still there—they're so terribly important. But—" he touched her lips with a fingertip, requesting permission to continue "—I didn't know what to ask, and you couldn't bring them up. Yesterday was a series of shocks, one after another, and I was obviously unprepared for any of them."

She didn't know what to say or do, yet fretted that her stillness might make him think that she didn't care enough to help him through this quandary.

"This morning, in the light of day, I realize what a lot we must discuss." Warmth began to kindle in his eyes. "I do love you, Andi, as much—even *more* than before, if that's possible. Your coming to find us, your wanting only what's best for us—these are far more than most would do.

"I didn't sleep much last night, but came to the conclusion that if marrying you means moving and changing my job, I can handle that. Most people do that in their careers, often with far less impetus—for money or position only." He pushed back hair from his forehead. "Which is what many will suspect I'm doing."

"Would that trouble you too much—what others think?"

"No one enjoys being judged harshly by others." There was a little crooked smile. "I definitely don't want to sound like a martyr, but leaving what I am isn't quite as easy as some might think. However, I'm convinced that, together, we can do it. And I'll sincerely try to be of help to you and your father in any way I can."

She felt the smile on her face and it was by sheer will that she remained on her side of the seat. "You will be, Keith."

"Want to give me some clue as to how I might fit in?"

"Well, you were fascinated by Research and Development. Would you like to try that?"

"So it's as simple as that?"

It was worse than overhearing co-workers refer to her as "the boss's kid." Her breath sucked in sharply. "I didn't mean to offend you."

He slid over to encircle her shoulders with an arm. "I need to apologize again. It's just—I've found my own jobs ever since I was sixteen and began stocking shelves in a grocery store. I never expected a dream job to be handed to me on a golden platter. For just a moment, I felt like a gigolo—being paid for marrying you."

He must have seen her dismay, for he added quickly, "I know you didn't mean it that way, dear. This is *my* problem only, not yours. I never before realized how weak I am."

They spoke of many other things, and finally he asked that they pray together, here in the rose arbor—

the first time for just the two of them. And she unexpectedly felt unbounded appreciation for him—and for God.

Afterwards, he could hardly get words out. "Having you as my wife will be such a blessing, Andi. I want to be with you always. I need to be. And as it says in the Bible, and in the marriage ceremony, 'a man shall leave his father and his mother and be joined with his wife.' Believe me, Andi, I can work at any job, anywhere, as long as I can come home to you."

"Oh, Keith, my darling." She was filled with joy and relished being in his arms where she belonged. And yet she asked once more, "You're sure? *Really* sure?"

"Forever and ever...."

Announcements of their engagement appeared in Chicago's and Dalton's society pages, as well as *The Sylvan Falls Herald* weekly shoppers' guide. Keith handed in his resignation as of the end of November, and spent as much free time as possible working on his house, though still undecided as to renting or putting it on the market.

Andi concentrated on her stint in R & D, finding one aspect of it especially fascinating—exhilarating. She always drove to work herself, instead of riding with Dad. She'd become too involved with projects to leave till late—and often continued working at home, using her own computer, into the early morning.

She also flew to Sylvan Falls many weekends, staying with Gram, who treated her even more lovingly than before. As did Karlyn. And Zack.

With others, things were less relaxed. Andi surmised this was at least partly due to resentment because Keith, so important a part of their world, would soon be leaving with her.

Paula invited her to the Susquehannock Hotel restaurant for a tastefully prepared and beautifully served luncheon, the one time Andi stayed over for a long weekend. But as soon as they'd finished their scrumptious Chocolate Vienna Torte, Paula rushed back to meet with a client.

Andi found Keith applying white paint to the woodwork of one of his front bedrooms one cloudy, humid Saturday in early September. "I thought you planned to strip this down to natural wood, not cover previously painted surfaces with another layer."

He looked around the large room with its bed, dressers and armoire pulled away from the walls. A momentary expression of longing crossed his face, but his words were matter-of-fact. "There's no time for that. And whoever rents or buys this property probably won't have the same love for chestnut that we do."

He can't bear to speak of it as his home! she thought sadly. She covered her clothing with an oversize old shirt and helped with the painting, especially appreciating this time alone. When they were out of town, wherever they ate, shopped or strolled, people stopped them to offer congratulations and best wishes, ask questions, or just visit. Keith welcomed each of them, giving as much of himself to an elderly man in a ragged shirt and less-than-clean bib overalls as to a young woman from his Sunday School class, and to several teens they'd met in a pizza shop just today at lunchtime, one of whom she remembered. "I want to thank you again for the mincemeat pie you brought me during the carnival, Rocky."

His feet shuffled and shoulders rose almost to his reddening ears. "It was nothing."

"It meant something to me. That pie was delicious!"

She asked how long he'd been a Junior Fireman and what he did there, so he spent several minutes talking about that before blurting out, "We're gonna miss Keith something awful when he leaves!" Turning toward him, the boy pleaded, "Do you *hafta* go to Chicago? Why can't you guys live here?"

There was a several-heartbeats-long pause before Keith said, "It's not possible, Rocky. My lovely soon-to-be wife has too many responsibilities there."

"But you have responsibilities here!" Rocky pleaded. "Aren't you gonna miss us? And your life here?"

Keith's deeply drawn breath gave him time to formulate his response. "Yes, I will miss all of you and what I've been doing but—" he reached for Andi's hand "—wait until *you* fall in love with a wonderful woman. Then you'll understand."

She was reminded of King Edward's renunciation of the crown of England in order to marry the woman he loved, and she felt humbled for asking so much. It must be difficult to have no more positive a response than a smile to Rocky's parting plea. "Think of *something* so you can stay."

They didn't refer to that while finishing the wood-work in the first room and starting the one across the hall. But other things—questions about *his* being a Junior Fireman, how old he'd been, and what his du-ties were, seemed to be safe ground for discussion.

"My grandfather pushed that program through shortly after becoming chief—before I came along. And it's paid off. Many of our firemen, men *and* women, started that way."

"Were you as close to him as to Gram?"

There was a long enough pause that she looked around. He was standing there, paintbrush unmoving against the wall. "He was one of the most important people in my life. I loved him more than almost any-one."

"I've hesitated to ask Gram, but a woman at the variety store said he died in a fire. I think she said it was—a mill burning?"

"A grist mill." He was looking out through the window, and she had the eerie feeling that he was seeing the past, not the present. "I was seventeen—nearing the end of my second year as a Junior Fire-man. The fourteenth of August. By the time the alarm was given and we got there with the fire equipment—and it was only four blocks away—the whole place was on fire, flames shooting through the wood-shingle roof and out the windows. Everyone knew there was no chance to save it, but we had to try. We always do." He turned, agony still evident on his face, un-dulled by passing years. "Grandad's first concern was making sure nobody was inside, and he was told that since it was a Saturday afternoon, no one was work-ing.

"But then Mrs. Carstairs came running down the street, screaming for her husband. They were the owners, as his family had been for four generations. It turned out he *had* come to do office work. And didn't return.... The assistant chief, Bob, said he was going in to find him but—" Keith could hardly continue "—there were flames everywhere, and the roar of them and of the people and the equipment and water..."

Should I stop him? Andi wondered. This is so hard for him—and I don't need to know. However, if he'd been so traumatized that he still could barely speak of his grandfather, perhaps he needed to continue.

"I ran for Grandad, wanting him to stop Bob from entering that inferno. And he did, physically dragging him out, and telling bystanders to hold him, if necessary. Mrs. Carstairs was hysterical, wanting to go in herself if no trained person would try to save her husband. And it was then that I saw Grandad in the doorway, flames behind and around him! *Everywhere.*

"He was looking right at me, Andi. He gave me a smile and a thumbs-up, like he'd done many times— when I made that home run in the Little League tournament, when I finished my solo in the Christmas cantata, when I showed him my report card saying I'd achieved High Honors.... And—then he was gone."

Andi shuddered, remembering Lois saying his body was found covering that of the other man, trying even at the end to give protection. But Keith was ashen, his face contorted with pain almost more than could be borne.

Laying her brush across the top of her can of paint,

Andi wiped her hands and left the unfinished window frame. Her arms went around him and she pressed as close as she could to his rigid body. "I'm sorry, Keith. So very sorry!"

"I can see him now, with that thumbs-up—especially for me. And those yellow and brownish-red, all-consuming flames."

His arms tightened convulsively, and she couldn't have pulled away had she tried. "He *had* to know he had little chance of getting back out, yet he gave me that thumbs-up.

"I tried to follow him—to help him there or make him come out. But others held me, kicking and screaming.

"And—" his voice was thick, scratchy "—I still wonder if maybe I could have saved him."

You've grieved about that all these years, blaming yourself for his death! "Do you honestly think that was possible, Keith?"

His head raised and he pulled away enough to look into her eyes. "Everyone says it wasn't. But perhaps, if I'd been braver. Tried harder. Torn away from them..."

She found herself praying for guidance, for words to help, but had no assurance that she was handling this well. She asked, "What does that thumbs-up mean to you?"

Raw grief was replaced only partially by the necessity of answering. "Approval, mostly," he replied.

"Since you knew him so well, which do you believe he meant right then? You can't think that he was encouraging his beloved grandson to follow him into the flames, can you?"

His slow exhalation was warm against her ear. "That—would have been totally out of character."

His eyes still held their pain, though his muscles seemed less spastic. "Could it have meant he appreciated your coming for him when the other man was going inside? That he was—commending you for saving *that* man's life?"

"But I wouldn't have called him had I known how he'd respond. He didn't deserve to die like that!"

"But you weren't the one to make that decision, Keith. He, of all people, knew his chances, and deliberately laid down his life in the attempt to save a friend."

A shudder passed through him, shaking her as well. "I still have nightmares...."

"Recently?"

"Not often, but—" his reluctance was obvious, then he nodded slowly "—yes."

She didn't have the courage to ask if this had happened since he'd known he'd be leaving. Could she bear it if that answer, too, was in the affirmative?

Some time later, he asked, "You're positive you want to be married here, not in Chicago?"

"This will be better for my Pennsylvania cousins," she said, remembering how she used to bunch them together that way.

"They're more than willing to travel."

"And I want them to come, many times. But your church means more to you than mine to me. And it was here that I again came close to God, through you and Gram and Karlyn, so it will be more meaningful for me to walk down this aisle in Mother's wedding gown. To come to you there.''

He did not argue this—nor anything else. That seemed nice at first, but she was beginning to wonder if he had no opinions on these subjects, or if he considered it the bride's prerogative to handle all wedding plans.

Or—and this thought was almost frightening—was he no longer discussing things that *did* mean something to him? Could he be overwhelmed by her father's electronics and financial acumen, their home, their wealth?

Money! she thought, frustrated. Most covet it and spend huge portions of their lives in its pursuit, positive its acquisition will bring unending happiness. If only they realized that the euphoric qualities attributed to great amounts of it are, like those for love, highly overrated. *Must* money always create problems?

Sunday morning. Church. With Gram on one side of her, singing soprano, and Keith on the other, Andi was filled with happiness as they harmonized several old gospel songs. But after sitting back down, she realized this had seemed especially precious partly because she'd sensed a shadow of unease between Keith and herself this weekend.

Of course that could be due to a difficult situation at work. She forced herself to stop mulling over the personnel matter and pay attention to the sermon.

But she soon found herself envisioning how the church would look with her planned floral arrangements. And she must remember to ask if the church had large candelabra to stand on either side of the bridal party.

She again pulled her mind back to the present. Maybe she hadn't missed much, though, since he was speaking about The Golden Rule, and though she didn't recall many scripture verses she'd memorized as a child, she *did* know about doing for others what you'd like them to do for you.

She looked sideways at Keith; was that what he was doing? Being especially kind since she was working long hours all week and flying here so many weekends?

Glancing at the bulletin, she saw the sermon title given as "The Golden Rule *Trap*," which was perhaps different. She sat up straighter, determined to keep eyes and ears focused on the pastor. "I always buy the first asparagus of spring," he was saying, "no matter how expensive it is. I bring it home, my wife steams it, and we both say how good it is. It was only this spring, however, after *nine* years of marriage, that we discovered neither of us enjoys it. We ate it because each thought the other did.

"While visiting the Smithsonian's salesroom, I was fascinated by a necklace with an ancient blue-glass pendant. My wife admired others, but I bought *that* because I wanted her to have the one I thought extra special. However," he said, "I have yet to see her wear it—and why should she, if she doesn't like it?

"With the best intentions in the world, we often make assumptions based on our own view as to what's best for others. As parents, we *must* do this. What 16-year-old wants to get home by whenever the curfew is, or always wants to come to Sunday School and church? And what three-year-old is always receptive to eating his or her vegetables?

"As we mature physically, emotionally and spiritually, however, we should take time to study and get to really know those around us. Perhaps something other than what *you* like would better serve or please your relatives and friends. Have you prayed about and made every effort to learn what *is* best for them?"

The sermon continued, but Andi's thoughts remained on this point. I know you'd prefer staying, Keith, she thought, but I am needed back home—and there's no way I can commute forever.

And I can't ask you to, either.

But I must admit, I haven't studied, prayed about, and made every effort to do what is best for you.

The sermon ended and the congregation stood to sing the final hymn and receive the benediction. Keith had to remain for a brief meeting, so as she and Gram walked back to the house, Andi shared her concern about yesterday's conversation.

Gram's head was tilted forward, as though she had to give full attention to where she placed each step. "That was such a terrible time for all of us! In my own grief, I was not even aware of the help he apparently needed."

Andi squeezed her hand in silent sympathy, and Gram murmured, "Come to think of it, he never speaks of that day, always changes the subject. I'm—grateful he told you."

They were crossing the street when she added, "I never knew of that thumbs-up gesture, which was so typical of Phil. It makes me wonder whether, as busy as he always keeps himself, Keith might still be trying to carry his grandfather's share, along with his...."

They went to Karlyn's in the afternoon, when Andi explained she'd like to play a game with the children. "This whole project is *very* hush-hush," she emphasized to Keith, indicating the computer disk she'd brought. "Some of us in Research and Development have been working day and night to get this and other disks ready for the big testing—using age-appropriate children. Since Jake and Traci are already so skilled on the computer, I especially want to see how well they'll do."

Both the seven- and five-year-old, having done this sort of thing for years, were fascinated with trying to get four lost children out of Bullfrog Swamp, over almost impossibly rigorous paths, and through or around ponds, thickets, patches of poison ivy, and other named and pictured obstructions. Depending on interactive choices, they could be helped by friendly animals, including birds and butterflies—or put in danger from others.

On the way back to Gram's, Keith commended her company on the product—and was impressed to find that this was what she'd been working on during her stint in R & D. "And," she added with a sigh, "much of my time at home, as well, for it's addictive.

"Chuck Enders, one of our brilliant young physicists, is in charge of this section. He had created, on his own time, several relatively simple games for his three- and four-year-old. At first it was just for fun— a break from what he was working on in the labs— but he's now so enthusiastic about the possibilities that a number of us, including me, are on the project full time.''

There was little opportunity for serious conversation or introspection after that, and time flew until she was driving the rental car back to the airport. She did not read while waiting for her flight; she just sat near the window, staring out almost unseeingly, thinking about the sermon.

No one could doubt that the Golden Rule was an excellent pattern to follow—but the Golden Rule *Trap* was an entirely different thing!

Keith had felt honored and pleased by his company's offering him that huge raise and stock options if he'd stay—even though knowing he couldn't accept it. He did not indicate to her any resentment or unwillingness about going.

She should be overjoyed at that, she told herself.

He said Tiffany had finally been taken to her adoptive home, and he'd informed the staff that he'd be unavailable to help with future crack babies. The only concern he'd expressed to her was that there might not be a volunteer to assist the next one.

By the time she was in the middle of her Pittsburgh layover, Andi almost wished she'd asked for a company plane. She never used them for other than business purposes, and knew she wouldn't, but time dragged. Even her novel didn't hold her interest.

Well, Keith's minister had recommended prayer…but she'd hardly begun when a middle-aged woman sat down by her and started talking.

Chapter Seventeen

At first Andi tried being as unresponsive as possible without being rude. Then she nodded—yes, it was too bad the factory where the woman worked had closed down. And it was tough that her husband's emphysema was so bad that he was now on disability.

Sue Heberling was on her way to Tulsa, Oklahoma, to care for two preschool grandchildren now with neighbors; their mother was in the hospital with an emergency appendectomy and peritonitis. Her flight would be leaving later than Andi's, but she not only asked for prayers, but wrote down her name and that of her daughter.

Andi took the assigned seat in her plane, beside a young woman in a slim, dressy suit. There was no actual communication between them, even after the plane was airborne, so there was no excuse now for not keeping her promise.

Being somewhat new at intercessory prayer, she gratefully recalled Gram's saying that she didn't consider it necessary to always close one's eyes. "Some of my most fervent prayers have been offered while behind the steering wheel—and I recommend open eyes then!"

Andi looked out over the top of the silvery wing, and prayed for Sue's daughter and grandchildren and for her ailing husband, who'd willingly sent his wife to help the others. *Please, God, help them, as only you can.* Knowing that wasn't enough, she then enumerated their needs as she knew them, praying for each.

Karlyn needed prayers, too, since her ex-husband had recently informed her that he was preparing to go back to court so he and his second wife could each have the two children half the time!

Andi had read of people praying for hours, and wondered how they could keep their minds disciplined enough for that. However, this time went by quickly as she prayed about specific problems and needs.

Thus far, she'd stayed with petitions on behalf of others, but now, while still in the air and not responsible for anything or anyone else, she prayed fervently for Keith and for herself. And for their relationship.

Help him to not be too sad about leaving his job and his fire company and his church and family. She was again struck by the enormity of everything that he was giving up. *It's not wrong to ask him to come to me, instead of it's working the other way, is it? You know how much we love each other—and you know how much Dad needs me. Please—if there is a better way, help us recognize what it is, and do it.*

It was then that the announcement came over the

speakers about seat belts being fastened and seats being returned to an upright position.

After landing, she picked up her car from the parking lot, and drove home through the not-too-congested traffic of early Sunday evening. Dad came from his den to welcome her, and she went there with him, which is where Carol brought large tossed salads, chicken-breast sandwiches and fruit.

"It does get exhausting," Andi admitted, kicking off her shoes. "Especially following such busy weeks."

"Perhaps it's time for him to take over some of the traveling," he suggested mildly.

That would be wonderful, she thought, but replied, "He's trying so hard to get his house ready for sale or rental. I suggested he hire someone for that, but he seems to like painting, and other fix-up chores."

She filled Dad in on the offered raise, and how things were going with the rest of the family. But then she went back to what they'd discussed before: her concern that Keith would miss what he was leaving behind.

Drew adjusted his recliner to a more comfortable position. "Is he complaining about it?"

"Not at all—which is one reason I feel so guilty— no, that's not quite the word." But she could think of none better. "I've been praying for wisdom to find another way."

The thinking lines across his forehead kept her silent. He suggested, "Let's sleep on it, princess."

When he asked in the morning if sleep had helped, she said, "I've got ideas, but you'll have to determine how good they are."

He listened without interruption as she reminded him of the most recent meeting of department heads, when Chuck Enders had once more brought up the formation of a totally dedicated Education and Game Division.

Most thought this had merit—for some time in the future. Their major argument against considering it now was that their facilities were already used to capacity, and there seemed no possibility of buying nearby land.

"He reminded us of how dependent we already are on instantaneous electronic transmission. Otherwise, department heads would be running the corridors all the time. He felt that this makes it possible to consider having the new division anywhere in the area."

Her father smiled wryly, guessing where she was heading. "And you're suggesting we expand that search area beyond the city's environs—perhaps to a town in north-central Pennsylvania?"

She smiled gratitude for his trying to make this easy for her. "Remember when we walked in the park there, and you asked about those huge brick buildings at the edge of town?"

He nodded. "You said a furniture factory went bankrupt and the creditors sold off everything but the property."

"That happened perhaps two years ago. They might be open to negotiating—should you think it's worth checking."

He sat there quietly for a moment. "Before I mention it to anyone, let's have Keith—and whoever in his company handles such things—look into the current situation. Space, soundness of buildings, layout, parking facilities, acreage, utilities—and especially its legal status and possible liens against it. And what about taxes? Do they offer incentives to companies moving into the area?''

She was again impressed by the efficiency of Dad's mind as he processed this new idea and came up with even more considerations, such as the labor situation. "Employees here would, of course, have opportunity to transfer, but are there many skilled workers already in the area? How do graduates of local colleges and technical institutions compare with those from Georgia Tech, RIT, and others?''

She got to her feet, eager to call Keith, but Dad laid a restraining hand on her arm. "One thing more, Andi—would this mean you'd want to stay in Pennsylvania all the time?''

She took her seat again. "Things would have to be worked out, but I believe it *is* doable. Since Chuck's the one pushing hardest for a new division, and since he knows most about it, he's probably the logical one to head it up.

"*If* he'd do that, and if we can get as efficient and personable an office manager as you have, I could be here several days, and there a day or two plus weekends.

"Once Jon died, I didn't complete the work necessary to get my pilot's license—but I *can.* If I have use of a company plane, the traveling shouldn't be a problem, and I'd always be available by phone, fax, or Internet.''

* * *

Andi was delighted with Keith's enthusiasm for the possibilities as she presented them. "Oh, Andi, that would be so wonderful. Sylvan Falls has been hurting without that factory. This could give us the boost we need!"

Dear, selfless Keith! Andi thought, her heart swelling. Thinking of the community even before his own emotional and family ties. "How long would it take to gather all that information?"

"Well, our architects did the plans for and supervised their expansion about ten years ago, so we have all those facts and figures in-office. And since scuttlebutt has it that creditors are screaming for their money, I'll make every effort to get things taken care of fast. They *could* be about to force sale of the factory itself, as they did before with the machinery and contents—which went for next to nothing at sheriff sale."

He laughed. "And as of right now, my love, I'm going in to personnel and tell them I might be withdrawing my resignation—and reminding them of that offer they made to keep me here."

Epilogue

Three years later

It was 4:37 p.m. on the thirteenth of October when seven-pound-seven-ounce Katherine Michaela Mc-Henry was for the first time placed in her mother's arms by her father who had, seven hours earlier, rushed to the hospital from his large corner office at the Dalton Design Group Building. Andi's labor and delivery had been difficult, but even though exhausted, she marveled, "Oh, Keith, she's so beautiful."

"She certainly is." One hand cradled the infant's head as he leaned over to kiss his wife. "And so are you, Andi. So are you, my darling!"

Gram couldn't come until evening, since Vanessa, McHenry Division's invaluable office manager and executive secretary, was needed at the plant. Sales had been even greater than projected, and orders and reorders from around the world had to be attended to immediately because of Christmas.

Vanessa left the office only ninety minutes late, after sharing the news of the baby's birth with her dad. Brad had proved to have remarkable abilities in sales and was often overseas. She hurried to take over supervisory duties at Gram's big old Main Street home. Along with a large grant from Drew, it had been Vanessa's organizational skills and Paula's handling of legal matters and meeting of all codes and requirements that made it possible for five unmarried pregnant girls to live here.

Drew, having kept a company plane on standby, left Chicago as soon as he received word that Andi was in the late stages of labor. He got his first look at his auburn-haired granddaughter at her mother's breast, with Keith on the side of the bed, encircling them with his arms.

Andi saw the tears running down her father's cheeks as he came toward them. Smiling her welcome, she reached to draw him close. "Hi, Grandpa. Come meet our next generation."

Family—how wonderful it is! she prayed.

I do thank you, God.

* * * * *

Dear Reader,

As with most writers, I have been an avid reader since childhood. Being by myself tending chickens and gathering eggs on our poultry farm, I'd occupy my mind with making up stories and playing with "what ifs." What if the author of that book I just finished had changed what happened *there*, what then would take place?

I was sure that someday I would write a book, a *romance*, because I especially enjoyed reading them. So I developed characters and places and wrote a lot— but it took many years and hundreds of published stories, articles and poems before I saw my name on the cover of a book. And the thrill of that keeps growing, *A Family for Andi* being my sixth novel.

In the meantime, I married a wonderful Christian man and we have three now-grown children, each deeply involved in a church and, more importantly, having a Christian home and family, where personal faith flourishes in everyday life.

If you have dreams, don't lose them, whether they involve writing, or painting, or climbing mountains or doing needlework. Without dreams, we accomplish little; with them, only God knows how far we can go. Just remember that on your life journey, you can have no better navigator than the One who created all things, including you.

Eileen Berger